Gage was a ... **the stairs** ... **swivelled ar**... **her searchingly.**

Then, as though he was acting on the spur of the moment, he pulled her to him and kissed her briefly—a swift, demanding kiss that took her breath away and left her senses in uproar. Her blood was surging through her veins, rampaging through every part of her, as though she was being taken by a storm.

He dragged his mouth away from hers and looked into her eyes. 'Goodbye, Amelie,' he said. 'Take care.'

She stared after him. Her lips were tingling with the sheer exhilaration of those stolen moments and her mind was in turmoil.

All her doubts came rushing back full force. He was going away for two whole days and she didn't have the first idea how she was going to cope. She had grown so used to having him around, but now he wouldn't be there when she most needed him. What was she thinking of, letting him into her heart?

When **Joanna Neil** discovered Mills & Boon®, her life-long addiction to reading crystallised into an exciting new career writing Medical Romance™. Her characters are probably the outcome of her varied lifestyle, which includes working as a clerk, typist, nurse and infant teacher. She enjoys dressmaking and cooking at her Leicestershire home. Her family includes a husband, son and daughter, an exuberant yellow Labrador and two slightly crazed cockatiels. She currently works with a team of tutors at her local education centre to provide creative writing workshops for people interested in exploring their own writing ambitions.

Recent titles by the same author:

THE LONDON DOCTOR
HER BOSS AND PROTECTOR
THE EMERGENCY DOCTOR'S PROPOSAL
THE CONSULTANT'S SPECIAL RESCUE
IN HIS TENDER CARE

HER VERY
SPECIAL
CONSULTANT

BY
JOANNA NEIL

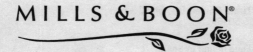

MILLS & BOON®

First published in Great Britain 2006
Harlequin Mills & Boon Limited,
Eton House, 18-24 Paradise Road, Richmond, Surrey TW9 1SR

© Joanna Neil 2006

ISBN-13: 978 0 263 84762 8
ISBN-10:   0 263 84762 4

Set in Times Roman 10½ on 12¾ pt
03-1006-50569

Printed and bound in Spain
by Litografia Rosés, S.A., Barcelona

HER VERY
SPECIAL
CONSULTANT

CHAPTER ONE

'YOU need to go now...go quickly. It isn't safe for you here.'

'But my dad...I can't leave my dad...'

Amelie struggled to recall what had happened to the little boy after that. She remembered holding his hand and helping him up the winding cliff path, urging him not to look back because it had seemed vital at the time that he didn't linger.

The situation had seemed so desperate back then, but now, as her thoughts drifted off into a nebulous dream world, it all seemed so far away. What was it that had been so pressing that she felt she had to act quickly? Had her brother's child been in danger?

'Connor?' She mumbled his name and tried to focus her thoughts, but something distracted her...a sudden noise, maybe, or perhaps it was a movement, a faint stirring of the air around her, that had caught her attention.

She frowned and tried to open her eyes to see who it was who had disturbed her deep sleep, but her eyelids were as heavy as lead and they remained steadfastly closed. Not only that, but her chest was tight, as though her lungs weren't functioning properly, and she was suffocating, gasping for air.

Someone was saying something, but she couldn't quite make it out, except that it dawned on her that it was a man's voice. Was it her father? What would he be doing here?

She wanted to ask what was happening to her, but when she tried, the words strangled in her throat.

'I'm sorry,' the man said. 'I know this must be distressing for you, but we're doing all that we can to help you to feel better.'

Amelie made a small choking sound in the back of her throat. What did he mean? Why was everything such a muddle in her head?

'Just give us a moment while we get the tube out.'

She frowned. She didn't recognise the deep male voice. It was such a relaxing voice, smoothing over her senses like cream swirling on coffee, coaxing her to slip back into that peaceful, oblivious sleep once more, but something stopped her. She couldn't do that…could she? A feeling of urgency preyed on her mind, pushing her to wake up.

The boy… That was it… That was what was troubling her. What was his name? Jake—Jacob? She had desperately wanted to help him and his father, but she didn't know what had happened to them. All she knew was that the boy's father was in danger.

'There was something I…needed to do,' she muttered now, but her voice sounded croaky and distant. She coughed and tried to move a hand over her face, but her reactions were sluggish, and something was covering her mouth, getting in her way.

'You don't have to do anything at all. Just take it easy.'

She had to get him to understand. 'I said that I would take care of him.' She was still too weak to concentrate properly on anything, but she recalled Jacob's anxious expression, the way his lower lip had trembled. He was only five or six years old, just a couple of years older than Connor, and she wanted to gather him up and take him out of danger.

'But my dad's hurt,' he had protested.

'I'll stay with him,' she had told him, but even as she'd said it, her heart had been thumping and her mouth had been dry with misgiving because the sea had been rising far too quickly. It had already soaked through her flimsy cotton skirt. It had lunged at the rocks and everything that had stood in its way, and uppermost in her mind had been the thought that time was running out. Above all, she'd needed to go back down to the man who lay in the shelter of the cove so that she could tend to his injuries.

'Do you promise?' The child's voice quavered.

'I promise I'll do my best to keep him safe.' She felt her lips moving, but the sound was distorted, and her mouth seemed to have difficulty forming the words.

'Perhaps you had better not try to talk for a while.' The man spoke again, his words easing over her in a smooth and satisfying way that compelled her to take note. He must have reached out and touched her, because she felt what seemed like a comforting hand come to rest on her shoulder. She subsided, letting her worries melt away, because right now it was far less troublesome to give in and simply obey his command.

'We'll keep her on oxygen, and give her another dose of the nebulised bronchodilator.'

It was that calm, deep voice again. Who was this man who insisted on interrupting her dreams? She had to see him, to look at the face that went with those gravelly tones.

Amelie's eyelids flickered open. The lights were dim, but she could see cream-coloured walls and a curtain screen, and there was all manner of equipment around the bed. She blinked. Was that a monitor by the side of her—a cardio-respiratory monitor?

'So you're back with us at last? How do you feel? Can you remember what happened?'

Amelie looked towards the sound and stared up into a pair of fascinating grey-blue eyes that were studying her in an oddly curious kind of way.

Confused, she said in a halting tone, 'Who…who are you?'

He smiled. 'I'm Dr Bracken. Gage Bracken, the A and E consultant. You were brought into hospital earlier this evening.'

'Was I?' Her brow furrowed. Her throat felt scratchy and sore and she tried to swallow to relieve the discomfort, but found that it hurt to do that.

'You might feel a little uncomfortable for a while. We had to put a tube down your throat to help you to breathe, and we put in a nasogastric tube, too. We removed them just a few moments ago. The effects should start to wear off soon.'

She realised at last that the thing that was covering her nose and mouth was an oxygen mask. Moving it to one side a little, she said, 'I don't remember coming here.'

'I wouldn't worry about it too much. You were unconscious when you were brought in, and that was some time ago. What matters is that you're back with us now.'

She was silent for a moment, trying to take it all in. She guessed they must have brought her to the local A and E department at the hospital that was closest to her home. Turning her head a fraction, she glanced at the monitor. It showed her heart rate and respiration, and from the look of things she wasn't doing too well. Her medical training told her that her heart rhythm was disordered, and her oxygen level was none too good either.

Even so, she could perhaps lay the irregular heart rhythm in part at the doctor's door. He was way too good-looking for anyone's peace of mind. His hair was black and somewhat spiky, cut in a youthful, appealing style, and the outline of his jaw was angular and pleasingly masculine.

'Can you remember what happened to you before you lost consciousness?'

Amelie looked back at him. His manner was soothing, but even though she was weak and still suffering from the after-effects of all she had been through, she recognised that he was watching her carefully, assessing her the whole time.

'I was in the water,' she managed, thinking back, 'and it was taking me out to sea.' She coughed suddenly and struggled to get her breath for a second or two. 'I was so scared. I tried to swim back to shore...but the current was too strong for me.'

He nodded. 'Air Sea Rescue brought you to safety. I can imagine you must have been very frightened. You've been through a terrible ordeal, and you're lucky to be alive. I do believe the worst is over, though, and that you'll be back on your feet before too long.'

The doctor studied her fleetingly as though he was

debating her state of mind. He said on a cautious note, 'When you were semi-conscious, you were trying to say something. It seemed as though you were worried that you should be taking care of someone…a child, I think…and you mentioned the name Connor. Is there anyone we should contact about him?'

'No, I don't think so.' She wasn't thinking too clearly, but she remembered Nathan telling her that he would be taking a break for a few days. 'Connor's with his father. They've gone away for the weekend, but they should be back some time tomorrow.'

He inclined his head a fraction and seemed to relax. 'That's all right, then.' Giving her a brief smile, he added, 'Perhaps you should try to get some rest now.'

He turned to move away, and she was swamped by a moment of panic. Was he really going to leave her alone here? She wanted to call him back, and her lips parted in readiness to speak out, but just at the last moment something stopped her. Her feelings of self-esteem came to the fore. She couldn't give in like that to feelings of desperation, could she? That wasn't her way at all. Hadn't she learned that it was better for her to try to be independent and not to expect help from anyone? Hadn't her father ensured that lesson had been driven home?

Amelie sank back against her pillows and tried to recover some of her strength. She felt like death, washed-out and drained of energy. At the back of her mind there was a sense that there was something she needed to do, but she couldn't quite remember what it was and the effort of finding out was all too much for her at the moment.

The doctor didn't return, but a nurse came to her

almost immediately. 'Hello,' she said. 'I'm Chloe. I just need to check your blood pressure and temperature.' When she had finished, she noted down the results on a chart, along with the recordings from the monitor.

She was a cheerful girl, pretty, with a friendly expression, and brown hair that was tied neatly back from her face and held within a simple band. 'How are you feeling?' she asked.

Amelie's expression was wry. 'A little rough, but I'm OK.'

The girl smiled at her. 'You should begin to get your strength back, bit by bit, from now on. When you're feeling a little better, we'll need to get some details from you. So far, we don't even know your name.'

'I'm Amelie. Amelie Clarke.'

'Is there anyone you'd like us to get in touch with for you, Amelie?'

Amelie thought about that. 'There's no one I can think of. My brother's away at the moment.' It would have been comforting to see Nathan, but he was with his girlfriend, Emma, and she knew they had planned on taking Connor to a seaside village further along the coast.

'Is there anyone else we could call? I imagine you'll need someone to bring some things in for you. You didn't have a purse or any belongings with you when you were found.'

'Oh.' Amelie's mouth straightened. 'I hadn't thought about that.' She suddenly realised that she had nothing of her own with her, not even her clothes. Looking down, she saw that she was wrapped up in a space blanket, designed to stop the patient from losing heat. 'I don't know what to do,' she said. 'I've only just moved to the area. I don't really know anyone yet.'

'Is there a neighbour, perhaps? Or we could arrange for someone to go over to your house to collect some things for you, if you like.'

That sounded like a reasonable compromise. 'I do have a neighbour. He might be able to sort things out for me,' Amelie agreed, relieved that they had found a solution at last. Her brother's friend lived in the cottage next door to hers, and maybe, if he was home, he could get hold of her spare key and bring some things in for her.

'I think we can arrange that for you.'

'Thank you.' Amelie frowned. 'Surely I must have had some belongings with me?'

Chloe shook her head. 'I imagine they were lost at sea. The incoming tide can throw up some fierce waves around these parts.' She glanced at the monitor, which had started to bleep a warning. 'Your oxygen level's a bit low. Time to start the nebuliser, I think.'

Perhaps it was the nurse's comment about the sea that stirred up fragments of memory in her, because all at once Amelie's mind was filled with frightening images of the rising sea, venting its spleen with powerful waves that dashed against a jutting peninsula. She recalled waiting with an injured man, watching fearfully as the water rose, coming ever closer to the cliff ledge where she sat, huddled. The incoming rush of water had rapidly obscured the strip of yellow sand that separated one cove from another.

'Are you all right?'

Amelie gave a small start and jerked her attention

back to the nurse, who was looking at her with a concerned expression.

'Yes, I think so.' She wasn't sure any more what was real and what was simply a figment of her imagination. It had seemed as though she had sat for ages beside the man on the ledge of the cliff, waiting for the rescue team to arrive, and all the time the sea had been thrashing her with all its might.

She said carefully, 'I keep seeing pictures in my mind, of the sea and the cliffs. It's horrible, like a nightmare.'

'That will probably keep happening to you for a while, but I'm sure it will pass, given time. You've had a bad experience.' The nurse started to prepare the nebuliser.

'Yes, I suppose that's true.' Amelie's brows drew together. In the end, the sea had won the battle, snatching her away from the ledge and dragging her into its fearsome, angry embrace. The water had swirled around her, tossing her this way and that, and it had been cold, chilling her through and through. A powerful undercurrent had tugged her steadily away from the shore, dragging her down, so that the effort of staying afloat had become altogether too much for her.

'Do you know if a little boy was brought in from the beach?' she asked, 'and was there a man who was injured?' Her mind was racing as a vision of the boy and his father came back to haunt her. Had the boy managed to scramble up to the top of the cliff?

The last Amelie had seen of the child had been a flash of his blue denim jeans as he'd headed up the last bit of the winding path that led upwards, away from the beach. She had caught a glimpse of his white trainers above her, and then the roar of the sea had drowned everything out, grabbing her attention once more. 'I need to know if they're all right.'

The nurse paused, frowning. 'I haven't seen anything of a boy, or heard of one being admitted. Who is he?'

'I don't know his full name. Jacob, I think. He was on the beach and I saw him go up the path to the cliff top, so perhaps I needn't have worried about him. There was a woman, too. Perhaps the woman took him home.'

The nurse looked at her blankly and Amelie added in a bleak tone, 'I don't know what became of them. I think the woman started up the cliff face but then the sea came in and washed everything away.'

'I don't know of anyone being brought in from the beach, but that could be because we've been taking care of you for the last hour or so. Certainly no one was brought in with you.'

Had she imagined it all? Amelie grimaced. 'I'm so mixed up,' she muttered. 'Perhaps it didn't really happen.'

'You shouldn't worry about it,' the nurse said gently. 'It's hardly surprising if you're feeling confused. You took a bit of a knock on your head and that might have caused you some problems.'

'Did I?' Amelie lifted a hand to her head. Her long chestnut-coloured hair was confined in part by a bandage, and there was a dressing of some sort at the back of her skull.

Chloe nodded. 'It isn't too serious an injury, but we think you were perhaps dashed against the rocks at some point.' She paused. 'Even so, to put your mind at rest, I'll see if I can find out who has been brought in recently. It might be that they've been taken to a different section.'

'Would you do that for me? Thank you so much.'

* * *

An hour or so later, Amelie was getting restless. Chloe hadn't come back to her, and she guessed that she had been called to deal with another patient, or maybe it was simply that there wasn't any news to tell. That made her worry all the more. Was she really so befuddled that she was concerning herself about things that hadn't actually happened?

Perhaps she should concentrate on getting out of here and going back to her normal, everyday routine. Seeing the nurses busy doing their work had reminded her that she was supposed to be starting a new job as a senior house officer in just a few days' time. She had wanted to prepare for it by doing some extra study, and bring herself up to date on some of the cases she might come across. How could she do that from a hospital bed?

She looked around for her clothes. They had exchanged the space blanket for one that was straightforward hospital issue, and she had been embarrassed to realise that she was wearing only her skimpy undergarments under a cotton hospital gown.

'Do you know where my clothes are?' Amelie asked a nurse, who was passing by the bed. There wasn't any need for her to wait here any longer, was there? No matter what condition the clothes were in, she could retrieve them, surely? Now that she was feeling a little better, all she wanted to do was to get out of there. There was no point in her taking up a hospital bed now that she was fully conscious, was there?

'I'm not sure what happened to them, but I expect Dr Bracken will know. We had to take your wet clothes off you so that we could get your temperature back to normal, you see.'

Amelie's face flushed with warm colour. Had Dr Bracken supervised her care the whole time?

The nurse shrugged a little. 'Anyway, I expect they're a bit of a mess by now. I wouldn't have thought they were in a good enough state for you to be able to wear them again.'

Amelie frowned, struggling to bring her thoughts back into gear. 'But what am I to do? I must have something to wear. I have to go home. There are so many things that I should be doing.' She was beginning to feel agitated all at once, disturbed by a sudden rush of concern over all the loose ends that needed to be tied.

The nurse looked at her oddly. 'I'm not so sure about that,' she murmured. 'Besides, we're still waiting to hear from your neighbour, as far as I know. I think Chloe said that he was out when she checked. Try not to worry. I'm sure we'll be able to sort something out for you.'

The girl moved away to the nurses' station, and Amelie was left feeling prickly and thoroughly out of sorts. She was unusually edgy, not used to being so dependent on others.

'What's this I hear about you wanting to go home?' Dr Bracken appeared at the bedside just a minute or two later, and directed a penetrating grey stare over her slender form. 'You must know that you're in no condition to be going anywhere, surely?'

Amelie winced under that stern gaze. 'I'll be all right, I'm sure. I feel much better now,' she protested.

'Maybe you do, but you're still not strong enough to think about going home just yet. You suffered a considerable shock to the system, and your heart rhythm is still erratic. Added to that, we have to be wary of lung complications. We need to keep you in here overnight at least, for observation.'

Amelie shook her head. 'I understand your concerns…really, I do…but I'm sure I shall be fine. I'm usually quite capable of looking after myself, you know, and you don't need to worry about me.'

His mouth made a wry twist. 'But I do worry, Miss Clarke.' He glanced at her left hand and must have noticed that it was bare of rings. 'It is Miss Clarke, isn't it?'

She nodded.

He pulled up a chair to the side of her bed and sat down. 'You see,' he murmured in a tolerant, understanding tone, 'you're my responsibility while you're here, and I'm not ready to take the risk of discharging you from my care. You'll have to forgive me if I don't share your optimism about your condition and your ability to cope.'

She stared up at him. 'That's because you don't know me,' she said quickly. 'I'm really very self-sufficient.' Unhappily, her grand statement was spoiled by a sudden coughing fit, which left her eyes watering and had her reaching for the box of tissues on the bedside table.

Dr Bracken beat her to it. Handing her a paper handkerchief, he raised a dark brow. 'Enough said, I think.'

When the coughing spasm was over, she slumped back against the pillows, trying to get her breath back.

The doctor regarded her thoughtfully. 'You see? As I may have already mentioned, you're in no fit state to be going anywhere.'

She was too winded to answer him for the moment, and he added dryly, 'Actually, I'm still not sure how you even came to be on the beach when the tide was coming in. Do you not know about high tide and the strong currents around here? Most people know enough about them to be very wary of the incoming sea.'

She swallowed. 'I'm new to this part of Cornwall. The day started out so fine that I thought I would just take a quick look around the place. I didn't mean to stay as long as I did.' Pausing for breath, she waited a second or two before tacking on, 'I hadn't seen the cove up until then, and I had it in mind to just spend an hour or so on the beach. I didn't really have time to stay any longer than that…what with moving in to my cottage, and so on.'

'And you're worried about getting settled in, are you?'

She nodded. 'Yes, that's right… And I'm supposed to be starting a new job in a few days. There are so many things that I have to do… I can't stay here and simply let them slide.'

He sent her a faintly amused glance. 'I'm afraid you're going to have to do just that. I'm inclined to think that your agitation is all part and parcel of what has happened to you, and if things are bothering you so much, perhaps we should consider medication as a way of calming you down. That way, we can make sure that you get all the rest you need.'

She stared at him, aghast. 'No way. You mustn't do that. I need to keep a clear head.'

'Then think of the alternatives. For a start, you could consider telling your employer that you've been involved in an accident, and that you'll be a few days late starting work.'

She shook her head. 'I can't do that. My new boss wouldn't be at all pleased if I don't turn up.'

'Are you sure about that? I really don't see that you have any choice in the matter. Your heart rhythm is all over the place, and your anxiety level is sky high, which isn't helping your blood pressure in any way. You need to stay here.'

'But you don't understand…there's so much I should be doing.'

He sent her a considering look. 'And how do you propose to leave here without your clothes? Were you planning on going barefoot, wearing just your cotton gown?' He shook his head. 'I suggest that you forget all about going home for the time being, Miss Clarke, and try to get some rest.' He paused. 'Of course, if it should prove totally impossible for you to do that, I'm sure I could find a way to ensure that you settle down.'

She stared at him. 'You wouldn't…would you?'

His mouth made a crooked slant, and his grey gaze flicked over her. 'Well, let's hope that won't be necessary.' He stood up then, in one lithe, fluid movement, and walked over to the nurses' station without a backward glance.

Amelie watched him go, her nerves thoroughly rattled by his confident, authoritative manner. She didn't want to be stuck here in this hospital bed, but he wasn't leaving her any alternative, was he? What choice did she have? She subsided against her pillows and glared at him, her green eyes sparking with embers of smouldering frustration.

CHAPTER TWO

AMELIE'S head was aching, and her lungs felt constricted. She was supposed to be resting, but that was virtually impossible because she still couldn't rid herself of the picture of that small boy scrambling up the path, and of his father, white with pain, lying at the foot of the cliff.

Perhaps the nurse was right in saying that she was confused, but it all seemed so clear to her now, and she could see it in her mind as if it was real. She hadn't been able to take the man to safety by the route the boy had followed...the path had already been washed away and replaced by the incoming tide. The ground where he'd lain shelved down towards the sea, and her feeling of unease had grown as the turbulent waves had made steady inroads on the small patch of sloping beach that remained.

Amelie frowned. She had no idea what had happened to Jacob's father. Had the rescue team arrived in time? She'd called them, hadn't she?

Her thoughts on the matter came to an abrupt end as Chloe came and swished the curtain of the cubicle to one side. 'We're going to move you over to Recovery,' she said. 'It will be quieter for you there, and Dr

Bracken wants you to undergo some tests to make sure everything is as it should be.'

'Does he?' What kind of tests? Surely they would be unnecessary.

She was about to say as much, but Gage Bracken came and stood by the entrance to the cubicle, ready to supervise the transfer, and she clamped her mouth shut.

He cast a long glance over her, and her cheeks flushed with faint colour under that warm scrutiny. She probably looked a dreadful sight. Fly-away tendrils of her hair had drifted down over her cheeks, while the mass of her long chestnut hair was spread about her shoulders in wild disarray, a jumble of tangled curls. She would have given anything right then to have a brush or comb to hand, so that she could make herself halfway presentable, but as it was, she felt as though she was at a thorough disadvantage.

He, as before, was impeccably turned out, wearing dark grey suit trousers, minus the jacket, and his shirt was faintly chequered in subtle tones that were pleasing on the eye. His shoulders were broad, and his frame was lean and muscular. Right now, he was watching her with a brooding expression, not taking his eyes off her, almost as though he expected her to bolt at the first opportunity.

There wasn't much likelihood of that, she thought dryly. She felt as though the stuffing had been knocked out of her, and she wasn't exactly sure of the reason for that.

'Why do I need more tests?' she asked him. 'We both know what caused my problems, don't we?'

'That's true, but I want to check out your lungs,' he murmured. 'It's only a matter of a few breathing tests, nothing more exacting than that, and certainly nothing for you to be worried about.'

'I'm not worried. I'd just like to be able to get out of here, so that I can find out what happened at the beach. I was sure that someone else was hurt, and I can't believe that I imagined everything.'

'Yes, Chloe mentioned as much to me.' He gave a wry smile. 'I think we should concentrate our attention on you just at the moment, though. I want you to relax and save your breath. You're not out of the woods yet, and you need to preserve your strength.'

She wasn't about to argue with him. She sensed that it would be a complete waste of time to do that and, anyway, her mind was distracted as Chloe wheeled the bed out into the main thoroughfare of the A and E department, taking her through the double doors towards the next bay.

The doctor followed their progress, glancing at her chart as he walked alongside the bed.

'Where are you going?' A small voice rang out across the corridor, cutting into Amelie's reverie, and she turned her head a fraction to where the sound was coming from.

A little boy stood at the opening to what she guessed was a waiting room. 'Where are you taking her?' he asked the nurse. His voice quavered.

'To a place where she can rest.'

Amelie frowned. 'Jacob?' Was it really the boy from the beach? She strained to get a closer look at him. That would mean she hadn't been imagining things, wouldn't it? All those fraught images that had been crowding her mind had been real all along.

The boy stared at her, and she saw that his face was streaked with dried-up tears. 'Why are you here?' he said. 'Are you poorly?'

The nurse hesitated but Gage said briskly, 'Keep going, Chloe. I'll sort this little problem out.'

He turned to the boy and put an arm around his shoulders, leading him away. Amelie tried to pull air into her lungs, saying quickly, 'No wait… I need to talk to him.'

Gage shook his head. 'I'll take care of it. Go on, Chloe. I'll be with you in a minute or two.'

Amelie struggled with frustration once more. She needed to talk to Jacob, to find out what had happened to his father. More than anything, she wanted to tell him that she had done all that she could to help him. She scowled. Why had that man chosen to interfere?

She was still glowering when the doctor came back a moment later. Chloe wheeled her into a secluded bay and drew the curtains around the bed, and Gage Bracken approached as though nothing at all had occurred to halt proceedings. He put his stethoscope to his ears and laid the diaphragm on Amelie's chest, listening intently. Amelie feebly tried to swat his hand away.

'I wanted…to talk to him…' she tried to say, her tone fierce, and Gage looked at her thoughtfully, his gaze narrowing on her.

'A friend of yours, was he?'

'Yes, he was. We met on the beach and spent some time together…getting to know each other.' She sucked in a breath. 'I want you to take me back to him.'

His lips moved in a fleeting grimace. 'All in good time. I told you, I need you to rest and safeguard your energy.' Turning to the nurse, he said quietly, 'Let's see if we can get her sitting upright in a more comfortable position. Her lungs are becoming overloaded with fluid because of the salt water, and I need to reduce the congestion as quickly as possible. I'm going to give her frusemide to try to counteract the pulmonary oedema.'

Chloe nodded and began to alter the slope of the backrest, before rearranging the pillows. 'There,' she murmured, glancing at Amelie. 'Does that feel better?'

'Yes, but I really…need to…see the boy…' Her voice faded away on a wheezy note.

The doctor flicked a stern glance over her. 'You should sit back and let us do all the worrying,' he said. 'It seems to me that you're having enough trouble breathing, without adding to your problems by trying to take on anything else.'

Amelie glared at him, but for the moment it was beyond her to say anything at all. She was far too winded, and that puzzled her. Had she heard him mention pulmonary oedema? He made it sound as though she was ill, but that was impossible. She was never ill. She was just a little out of breath, that was all.

Gage Bracken moved briskly away before she could gather her resources together enough to question him, and she was left to cool her heels in bed for a while longer. Resentment bubbled inside her. It seemed as though the nurse was her only ally, but she was busy, checking up on other patients as well as monitoring Amelie's condition from time to time. Amelie had no choice over the next hour or so but to do as the consultant had ordered, to lie back and gather her strength.

Knowing that Jacob was safe was a huge relief to her, but it only brought more unanswered questions. He had appeared to be upset, and that could have come about for a number of reasons.

Had his father survived? Amelie and the man's female companion had managed to lift him up on to the cliff ledge, out of the way of the water, but help had been a long time coming. He had been groaning with pain, and his face had been white with shock.

'Can you scramble up the rest of the way to the top of the cliff?' Amelie had asked the woman. 'I'll stay here and take care of your friend, but someone should be with the little boy.'

The woman hesitated, torn between leaving the man and going to the child. 'I think so,' she said at last. 'I'll try.'

Had she made it? Amelie struggled to recall what had happened after that, but her head was throbbing, making it difficult for her to think clearly any more.

Eventually, Chloe came back to the bedside. 'How are you feeling now?' she asked.

'Much better,' Amelie told her. 'My breathing is a lot easier, so I think the medication must be doing its job.'

'That's good.' Chloe smiled. 'Is there anything I can get for you?'

Amelie shook her head. 'No, thank you. But perhaps you can tell me about the boy, Jacob? Did you manage to find out anything? Was his father admitted after all? I don't understand what happened.'

Chloe nodded. 'Apparently the coastguard picked him up, and when his condition was stabilised he was transferred by ambulance to us. He was badly injured and he needs surgery.'

'What about the boy—do you know if someone is taking care of him?'

'Yes, a nurse is looking after him. A woman came in with them, but as far as I know she didn't stay around for long.' Chloe lowered her voice. 'I gathered from what she said that she isn't the man's wife. She was with him, but she's married to someone else and she decided to make herself scarce once she knew that they were both in safe hands.'

That fitted in with what Amelie had expected. From one or two observations she had made during the course of the afternoon, Amelie didn't think that the woman from the beach was the child's mother. The couple had been too engrossed in one another to pay the boy much attention, and neither of them had noticed that Jacob had started to wander over the rocks towards the water's edge.

'So...are they trying to get hold of the boy's mother?'

'I believe so, but she's not at home. I think the little boy is quite upset.'

'I can imagine that he would be.' Amelie shifted restlessly against her pillows. She was unable to do anything, stuck here in this hospital bed, and her frustration was growing by the minute. If she could just to talk to Jacob, perhaps she could help to put his mind at rest. But was that possible? What if his father was in a really bad way? Despite her efforts, he had lost a lot of blood after all.

Even so, she couldn't simply lie here and do nothing. 'Perhaps I could do something to help to soothe him. He's so young, and he must feel that here he's surrounded by strangers...but at least he knows me, from the beach.' A note of agitation crept into her voice. 'I need to go and see him.'

Chloe frowned. 'I don't know about that. I'll have to

ask.' She moved away from the bedside, and Amelie's exasperation grew. No doubt she would tell the doctor that the patient was giving her trouble again, and Gage Bracken would find more ways to keep her in check.

Sure enough, he came to her cubicle a short time later. 'What's this I hear about you wanting to go over to the fracture unit?' he asked. 'Don't you have enough to occupy you, getting yourself back on your feet?'

'It's just that I was with the boy and his father—well, I mean, not with them—but I was there when the accident happened. I might be able to talk to the little boy and help him to understand what's going on.'

He studied her, his gaze moving slowly down from the top of her head and shifting over her slender form. She wished she knew what he was thinking.

'I can see that we're not going to be able to settle you down until you satisfy yourself that he's all right,' he said dryly. 'Are you always this determined to get your own way?'

'Only when it's important. Does this mean you'll let me go and see him?' Her eyes widened. She could hardly believe that he might actually be conceding to her wishes…he who was always so firmly in control. Perhaps she had better make a move before he changed his mind. Without giving it another moment's thought, she pushed the bed covers back and started to swing her legs out over the bed, pausing for a second or two as the room around her began to rock unsteadily.

'Oh, no, you don't,' he said in a terse voice, his hand coming out to grip her shoulder and hold her still. 'Just you stay where you are.'

'But—'

'But nothing.' He glowered at her. 'You will stay there while I go and get a wheelchair.'

So he wasn't going to hold her back. A kind of elation swept through her. At least the walls had stopped swinging around now, but her head was still off somewhere in the clouds. She leaned back against her pillows. That couldn't be anything to do with him touching her, could it? Strangely enough, she could still feel the imprint of his palm on her shoulder, and the warmth seeped through her thin cotton gown and fizzed along her veins like wildfire. She didn't understand it one bit but, then, perhaps she was running a temperature.

'Am I taking you from your work?' she asked when he came back and helped her into the chair. 'Perhaps there's a porter who could take me there?'

'I'll do it. I'm going off duty now, so it isn't a problem.'

She looked at him guardedly. Why was he putting himself out to go with her? Perhaps he simply wanted to make sure that she didn't get into any bother that could set back her progress so far.

'Did you say much to the little boy when you took him back to the waiting room earlier?' she asked. 'He seemed to be quite troubled.'

'Yes, he was. He told me that he was waiting for his mother, but that the nurse said she wasn't at home. He's not very happy at all, poor little man. His clothes are wet, so I gather he must have been in the sea at some point himself. Do you know anything about that?'

She nodded. 'He was climbing over some rocks, and then he waded out into the sea. He seemed to be going out of his depth, and then a freak wave came and caused him to tumble. He was shocked, but he managed to get back to the beach.' She frowned. 'He must be feeling cold and miserable, and tired, too, by now. After all, it's getting very late, isn't it? I thought perhaps the nurses would wrap him up in a blanket or something.'

'They did, and they gave him something warm to drink, but they were concentrating most of their attention on treating the father. I've asked them to see if they can find him something dry to wear. We usually have spare clothes in a cupboard somewhere for any children that are brought in.'

'That's good.' At least he had done what he could to make sure that Jacob was all right. She hesitated, waiting while he wheeled her towards the unit that dealt with fractures. As they approached an open doorway, she could see that the little boy was still in the waiting room just across the corridor, sitting at a table, colouring a picture. A nurse was with him, but she moved away as Amelie and Gage came into the room.

Jacob looked up at them. His face was pale, pinched looking, but he stared at Amelie, saying, 'I thought you was my mummy.' His shoulders hunched.

'She's on her way,' Gage said, his tone gentle. 'She went away for the weekend, to stay with a friend, because she thought you were going to be with your dad. It will take her a while to get here, but you shouldn't worry. She'll be with you before too long.'

'My dad broke his leg,' Jacob said. His mouth trembled. 'It was my fault. I made him do it.'

Amelie wheeled her chair closer to him and reached out to put her arms around the boy. 'No, Jacob, it wasn't your fault. You mustn't think that way.'

He looked up at her. 'But he came to get me, and that's when he fell down. He hurt himself on the rocks.'

'He twisted his foot and lost his balance because he was hurrying. You didn't do anything to make him fall. It was the rocks. They were slippery, and he caught his ankle in a small crevice. It wasn't anybody's fault. Sometimes these things happen.'

'You didn't fall down.'

Amelie smiled at him. 'That was just as well, wasn't it? Someone had to fish you out of the water.'

The boy looked down at his picture. 'I didn't like him being with Caroline. I wanted my mummy. I wanted my mummy and daddy to be together.'

'I know you did.' Amelie stroked his fair hair and tried to comfort him. What could she say that would take away the hurt? She knew what the boy had been going through. She recognised that vulnerability, that defeated slump of the shoulders that showed his acknowledgement of the fact that his world had been torn apart by his parents' separation, and things would never be quite the same again.

It had happened in much the same way to her and Nathan. One day their father had left their mother and their once safe world had crumbled. Perhaps the only difference between their circumstances and Jacob's was that it looked as though Jacob's father had at least been making an effort to keep in touch with his son. She had learned that much in the time that she had spent crouched on the ledge with him.

'Is my daddy going to be all right?' Jacob asked. 'I wanted to talk to him, but the doctor took him away and my daddy was just lying there and he wasn't saying anything to me.'

'I don't know,' Amelie said. 'I hope so. We can perhaps try to find out for you.' She turned to look at Gage, her expression serious. In a low tone, she said, 'I know he lost a lot of blood. Is there some way we can get to know how he is?'

He nodded. 'I'll go and make some enquiries. The last I heard the orthopaedic surgeon was taking him up to Theatre.'

'Thank you.' She hadn't expected him to go himself, but his willingness to help out was making her warm to him more and more.

He glanced at the boy. 'I'm sure the doctor's doing everything that he can to try to make your father well again. Stay here and talk to Amelie while I go and find out how he's doing.' He indicated to a nurse to watch over them, and left the room.

They waited, and Amelie talked quietly to Jacob, distracting him by showing him how to make paper aeroplanes from sheets of paper on the table. Then she helped him to draw colourful patterns along their wings.

They were still absorbed in this task when Jacob's mother arrived. Immediately, Jacob ran to her, flinging his arms around her waist, and she hugged him in return.

'It's all right, chick,' she said. 'It's all right. You don't need to be upset.'

Jacob sobbed, clinging to her, blurting out everything that had happened. 'His bone was sticking out,' he said, 'and it wouldn't stop bleeding.'

'Poor baby. Hush, don't cry. It's over now.'

'Am'lie bringed some little scissors out of her bag and she cut the beach towel up. She rolled bits of it up and put them on Daddy's leg, but the blood kept coming through. It was horrible, Mummy…it was horrible.'

'I know, Jacob. I know.' The woman's gaze met Amelie's over the boy's head. 'Thank you for helping,' she said.

'I wasn't sure how successful I was,' Amelie murmured. 'I couldn't splint the leg properly because there was nothing to hand, so I bound it to his good leg to minimise any damage when we moved him. The tide was coming in and we did what we could to get him out of the way of the sea, but it seemed that we had to wait a long time for help to come.'

'They told me Air Sea Rescue was out on another call.' The woman looked as though she was having trouble taking it all in. 'I'm just thankful that you were there with Jacob and his father.'

A faint sound interrupted them and Amelie turned to see that Gage had come into the room. She didn't know how long he had been standing there, but now he came towards them and said quietly, 'Hello, I'm Dr Bracken. Are you Mrs Collier?' He held out his hand to the woman in greeting.

'That's right. My husband broke his leg…he's been taken up to Theatre.'

'I know. I've just been talking to the surgeon and it appears that Miss Clarke probably saved your husband's life,' he murmured. 'An artery in his leg was damaged, and the blood loss was substantial. It could have been life-threatening if she hadn't managed to stem the flow.'

'That's what the nurse told me.' The woman bit her lip. 'Is there any news?'

Gage nodded. 'He has just come out of surgery. He's very weak, but I can tell you that the operation was successful.' He looked at Jacob. 'We think your daddy's going to be all right.'

Jacob sent him a beaming smile, while his mother closed her eyes briefly. When she had recovered, she asked, 'What did the surgeon have to do?'

'The break was a nasty one, involving both the tibia and fibula...that is, it involved both bones of the lower leg. The bones were displaced, which meant they had to be realigned, and then the surgeon had to pin them together with metal screws. I'm afraid it will take several months and possibly a good deal of physiotherapy before he's able to use the leg properly again.'

'As you said, he's lucky to be alive.'

Gage nodded. 'He's still coming round from the anaesthetic, and he's in a good deal of pain, but you'll probably be able to see him shortly, if you want to do that.'

'I think Jacob will want to see him to reassure himself that he's all right.' The woman sent Gage a quick, appreciative glance. 'Thank you for letting us know what's happening.'

'You're welcome.' His gaze went to Amelie. 'Do you want to stay here a little longer, or are you ready to go back to Recovery now?'

'I'm ready to go back,' she murmured.

He waited while she gave Jacob a quick hug and took her leave of Jacob's mother, and then he wheeled her out of the room and back towards the ward. Once she was settled in her own bay, he looked at her consideringly.

'I can see now why you stayed so long at the beach.

It wasn't by chance, was it? You put your own life at risk to stay with Mr Collier.'

'I didn't see that I had any choice. I was just alarmed that the rescue team took so long to get to us. I was beginning to think that neither of us would make it through the night.'

He nodded. 'The coastguard winched him up, but you had already been swept out to sea apparently. Mr Collier was taken to County Hospital, and as soon as he was stable enough, he was transferred over here.'

She was puzzled. 'But this is the County Hospital, isn't it?'

'No, in fact, this is the Royal West Country Hospital, not County.' He was frowning now. 'Why does the difference matter? Is it important?'

'Yes, it is…to me, anyway. I'm going to be an SHO at the Royal West…in the Emergency department. It's further for me to travel from where I live, but it's the biggest teaching hospital around. I didn't realise that I would be working here.'

'So you're a doctor?' He looked startled.

'That's right.'

'Ah, I see… Things are becoming much clearer to me.' His gaze narrowed on her. 'Now I understand how it was that you knew how to treat Mr Collier's injuries. You know all about A and E procedures.'

'Yes. Well, most of them. I haven't had extensive experience in Emergency work. I was hoping that I would get that during my SHO post.'

She stared at him, another realisation dawning on her. If she was going to be working here, didn't that mean that Gage Bracken was going to be her boss?

His gaze meshed with hers and she knew that the same thought had occurred to him, too. 'So you're going to be part of my team?'

'I... It certainly looks that way, doesn't it?' She couldn't tell what effect that knowledge had on him, whether he was pleased or dismayed.

A muscle flicked in his jaw. 'Well, Miss Clarke...Dr Clarke...all I can say is that for the moment you are still a patient in my care, and I hope that you will look after yourself and make a full recovery. That means you have to do exactly as you're told and be a model patient for as long as you're here.'

She gazed at him, wide-eyed. 'I can do that.'

'Hmm. I have my doubts, but we'll see about that.' He looked at her, his expression brooding. 'I don't want to see you at work until you are fully fit. Do I make myself perfectly clear?'

'Absolutely.' She would follow his instructions to the letter, once she had recovered from the shock of knowing that she was to work with him. There was no way she wanted to get on the wrong side of this man.

CHAPTER THREE

'BRMM…brmm…' Connor raced his toy car along the tabletop. 'Did you see that, Amelie? It goes well fast.'

'So it does.' Amelie looked at her four-year-old nephew with affection. Like his mother, he had light brown hair that looked as though it had been kissed by the sun, and his eyes were hazel, clear and bright. 'I want you to put your car down now, though, and finish up your cereal, or we'll be late for nursery school.'

She glanced at her watch. She was supposed to go to her induction meeting at the hospital this morning and time was running on. The last thing she needed was to be late on her first day, especially after the way she had been introduced to her new boss. He needed to see that she was fit and well, and on the ball.

Of course, she hadn't bargained on having to look after Connor, today of all days, but she had promised Emma that she would help out, and she didn't want to let her down. With Emma's mother in hospital, having tests on her heart, and Nathan away on a course, it wasn't as though there had been many options left.

'Daddy bought me a big car for my birthday,' Connor

confided, as he obligingly dipped his spoon into his breakfast bowl, 'but Mummy said I had to leave it at home. She said there wasn't no room for it in her car. It's this big and you can sit in it.' He spread his hands to show her.

'That is big.' Amelie laughed, and he nodded, picking up his mug and taking a long drink of milk. Then he grinned at her, a creamy moustache edging his upper lip.

'Grandma said it was fantabulous.'

'You're a lucky boy,' she told him, as she started to clear away the breakfast dishes. 'Didn't I hear that you went to the zoo with your grandma and grandad the other day? That must have been fun.'

He nodded. 'Yes. We saw some elephants and a lion, and some monkeys, and we had burgers and chips and we was going to go in the butterfly house but Grandma was cross with Grandad because he was moaning about my daddy and so we didn't.'

'Oh, dear. That's a shame.' It was no secret that Jacob's grandfather didn't approve of her brother, but she hadn't realised that his feelings had spilled over to the child. 'Were you unhappy about that?'

'No. I didn't really want to see the butterflies. I wanted to go on the climbing frame and the slide.'

She gave a wry smile. 'Well, perhaps you can do that another time, when your grandma is feeling a bit better.'

It was some fifteen minutes later that Amelie finally managed to get Connor into her car and off to school. As soon as she had seen him settled there, she drove to the hospital, disturbed because nothing was going smoothly this morning. She wasn't used to looking after a young child, and everything seemed to have taken so much longer than it should have. To cap it all, she had a struggle to find a parking place.

At last she managed to slot the car into a vacant spot that opened up and she locked up and then sprinted towards the main building. Now all she had to do was to find her way about the place. It was one thing knowing where the A and E department was, but quite another finding the room where the induction meeting was being held, and first of all she needed to go to the administration office.

Out of breath from her exertions, she wandered up and down the corridors. The place was like a warren, with passageways leading off here, there and everywhere, and she was sure she had already been down this one.

Harassed, she wondered how Gage Bracken would react to her turning up late, but perhaps he wouldn't be there today. The thought cheered her. After all, the meeting was for all newcomers to all departments, not just the A and E intake. Surely the consultant would have far more important things to do than to spend time acquainting his team with day-to-day procedural details?

Feeling brighter by the minute, she glanced around and saw a sign for the office where she was supposed to be.

In the office, a dark-haired, middle-aged woman glanced at her across the desktop, taking in the pristine appearance of Amelie's smart white doctor's coat and skimming over the cotton top and snug-fitting skirt that she wore beneath it.

'Hello, my dear,' she greeted Amelie. 'What can I do for you?'

'I'm here for the induction meeting, but I have to

collect a few items first. I believe you have them for me?'

'The induction meeting—you're a bit late, aren't you?' the woman said, glancing at the clock on the wall. 'And I can see that you don't have a name badge. You do realise that you were supposed to pick it up a couple of days ago, don't you?'

'Um—yes, but I've only just moved to this part of Cornwall. I'm still a bit at sixes and sevens, you see. I thought perhaps it wouldn't matter if I waited to collect it today.'

'Well, I suppose that explains it.' The woman grimaced faintly. 'It seems to me that a lot of you people are thinking the same way. We're overrun with students and junior doctors today, and none of you seem to know what you're supposed to be doing.'

Amelie wasn't quite sure how to respond to that. 'I imagine that's what the induction day is all about…to help us to get acquainted with everything.'

The woman nodded. 'What name is it?'

'Amelie Clarke.'

The woman consulted a list. 'Oh, you'll be on Dr Bracken's team, then.' She smiled and then hunted in a drawer until she found a badge that matched. 'You'll be all right with Dr Bracken. He's a remarkable doctor…very efficient and conscientious. Nothing's ever too much trouble for him.' Pushing the badge across the desk to Amelie, she said, 'There you are. Make sure you wear it at all times.'

'Thank you. I will.' Amelie pinned it to her lapel there and then, and saw that the woman was also wearing a badge, identifying her as Stephanie Baxter.

She sent her a quick glance. 'Shouldn't I have a time-table and a plan of the hospital, Stephanie, so that I'll be able to find my way around?'

'Of course you should.' Stephanie went over to a filing cabinet and came back with some papers, which she placed on the table in front of Amelie. 'There they are.' She frowned. 'Some people have already lost theirs. I do hope that you won't do the same. I'm running short of copies.'

'I'll look after them,' Amelie promised. She was far too aware of the minutes ticking by for comfort. She glanced at Stephanie. Was that it? Was she free to go on her way now? She started to turn away.

'Wait a moment,' the woman said. 'You don't have your hospital file, do you?' She made a rueful face. 'I did send everyone a list of items you need to have with you, but hardly any of the juniors seem to have consulted it. I sometimes wonder why I bother typing out these things.'

Amelie winced. There had been so many other, more important things to commit to memory, and she had tucked the printed sheet of paper in her bag out of the way, intending to glance over it while she had been on the beach the other day. It had been washed away, along with her other belongings.

'Wait there until I get it for you.' The woman shook her head. Clearly she'd had enough of junior doctors already.

Amelie looked down at the watch on her wrist. They must already be half an hour into the meeting by now. How was she going to explain herself?

'Here you are.' The woman searched the shelves behind her and then heaved a thick file down onto the

desk. Amelie stared at it. It was enormous. There must
be a thousand pages in it at least, she reckoned, her face
paling. Did she really have to read through all that?

'Please, don't lose it,' the woman said. 'I don't have
spare copies to give out.'

'I won't. Thank you.' Amelie scooped up the file and
hurried away, thankful to escape from there at last. Now
all she had to do was to hunt down the room where the
meeting was being held.

She found it just a few yards away, along the corridor.
Relieved that she didn't have to go back to the office to
ask the way, Amelie nudged open the door and went inside.

People were standing around talking quietly, and one
or two were helping themselves to coffee from a
machine. Relieved to discover that she probably hadn't
missed anything major, Amelie looked around for a
table where she could offload the heavy file.

Depositing it on a worktop by the door, she turned
and glanced about her. 'I thought I was going to be
late,' she murmured to a man who was standing nearby.
'Have I missed anything?'

'Not yet. We're a bit late starting—it seems as though
we all had trouble finding this place,' he said, 'and none
of us had the proper paperwork to hand.'

Amelie glanced at his name badge. 'Dr James
Malloy, House Officer', she read. He was young, with
a pleasant, friendly face and a mop of fair hair.

She nodded. 'There aren't enough signs to point the
way, and as to paperwork, I had to stop by the office
to collect mine before I came here. I probably wasn't
there for long, but it seemed like ages when I was

already late. There's so much paraphernalia to collect. It must weigh a ton.'

James smiled. 'You were held up there as well, were you? I had to sort out several details, and I think Ms Baxter was a bit taken aback that it wasn't as straightforward as it might have been. She asked several questions that I didn't have the answers for, and I was beginning to wonder if it was some kind of vetting process we had to go through.'

'Now, there's an excellent idea.' Gage's droll comment intruded on their conversation. 'I've always found my secretary to be a sound judge of character. Unfortunately, she has enough to keep her busy, without having to spend time and energy screening junior doctors.'

Amelie swivelled around and stared up into Gage's dark eyes. How could fate be so underhand? Why did he have to be standing there at that precise moment? Had either of them said anything untoward? She almost wanted a rewind so that they could do things differently.

She opened her mouth to say something and then thought better of it. Instead, she studied him. He was wearing an expensively tailored grey suit, teamed with a pale blue linen shirt, and he looked impressive, broad-shouldered, lean-hipped, vigour and strength emanating from every pore.

'Your secretary?' James frowned. 'The lady in the office is your secretary?'

Gage's glance moved over him briefly, his mouth taking on a wry slant. 'She is. Stephanie has had to stand in today for the duty clerk, and I think we should be grateful to her for doing that. She has more than enough work to do without taking that on as well.'

'We didn't mean to imply that there was anything wrong in the way she dealt with us,' James hurried to say.

'Of course you didn't. She's very good at what she does. I have to say that I find her to be extremely reliable and efficient.' His gaze shifted to encompass Amelie. 'That extends to the rest of my team. We work well together and I hope you'll both be an integral part of it.'

James nodded. 'I'm sure we'll do our very best.' He excused himself and made his way over to the far side of the room, where he merged into the small group of people assembled there.

Amelie watched him go and then turned to look at Gage. 'Perhaps I'm fortunate in having met some of the members of your team while I was in here as a patient. It wasn't the way I would have chosen to meet them, but I do appreciate the way they cared for me.'

His gaze moved over her. 'Are you sure that you're fully recovered?'

'Yes, I am. I'm in perfect health and ready to make a start.'

'Hmm…I hope that's true, for your sake. You had a very unpleasant experience, and sometimes there can be residual problems.' He looked her over once more, his glance shifting from her burnished shoulder-length curls, along the curving lines of her slender frame, all the way down to her sensible kitten-heeled shoes. Her face washed with warm colour under that assessing gaze.

He smiled faintly. 'You certainly look in good shape right now, at any rate. I saw you earlier, though, when you first came into the hospital. I was at the other end of the corridor, and it seemed to me that you appeared a little breathless.'

Amelie was startled to discover that he had noticed her before this. She blinked, and thought back to what had happened. 'That was because I was running late and I had a bit of a rush to get here,' she admitted. 'Then I had trouble parking. I'll need to get a permit for the car park, so at least that will be one less difficulty to contend with.'

He sent her a thoughtful glance. 'What was the problem today…apart from the parking? Was there anything in particular that made you late?'

His questioning flummoxed her for a moment or two, perhaps because she hadn't expected him to show an interest in her daily life. 'Only that I had to take Connor to nursery school, and it all took much longer than I expected.'

Gage gave her an odd look. 'I remember that you mentioned Connor when you first started to recover. You were very concerned about his well-being. I didn't realise…' He broke off, then added, 'It must be hard for you, having to cope with looking after a child and coming out to work, especially since this is your first day in a new job. Couldn't his father have helped you out?'

She shook her head. 'No, it just wasn't possible. He's away on a course for a day or so. He works at the Animal Rescue Centre, and he's trying to gain some extra qualifications.'

'I see.' He frowned. 'How will you manage to fit things in with your work in A and E? Is it going to make life difficult for you?'

'With Connor, you mean?' She sent him a swift look. Was he concerned that she might make a habit of being late? There shouldn't be any problems now that she had made a trial run, should there? Emma would be taking her mother for more tests at County early tomorrow morning, and again the next day, but after that she would be able to keep Connor with her. 'My shift pattern fits in with his early start at nursery school,' she said. 'It should work out just fine.'

'Let's hope so,' he said on a doubtful note. 'You must tell me if you think you might have any difficulties, and we'll try to work something out.'

It was thoughtful of him to offer to help out. She was about to tell him that there wouldn't be any more problems, though, since Connor would soon be back with Emma, but he flicked her a quick glance and said, 'It looks as though everyone has arrived now, so I should go and start the meeting.'

'Of course.'

He inclined his head a fraction and moved away from her. She watched him go and puzzled over the faint sense of reserve that had crept into his manner when she had mentioned Connor. Had she imagined it? She frowned. He surely didn't think that she was Connor's mother, did he? That would explain his caution, wouldn't it? Perhaps he was worried that being a single parent wouldn't fit in with her work in A and E.

The meeting started almost straight away, and Amelie dismissed the thought from her head. Everything went smoothly from then on, except that Amelie queried the schedule for her six-month stint and that meant Gage had to explain the allocated slots that had been set aside for tuition and progress reports.

'You won't all be following the same path,' he said. 'Perhaps we could deal with these individual queries later?'

'Of course. I hadn't realised that we each have a personalised schedule,' she murmured. Maybe he hadn't appreciated her interruption. From then on, she paid careful attention to what was said, and spent time getting to know her new colleagues. Some of them were going to be working in different departments in the hospital, but she and James were both assigned to Gage's team.

A couple of hours later, during a break, Amelie went to help herself to coffee from the machine. She put her notebook down on the worktop as she filled her cup from the filter jug, and when she had finished she sent a glance over the notice-board, idly inspecting the leaflets that had been pinned there. Among them was a note about the servicing of medical equipment, and it should have been innocuous, but as she inspected it more closely she felt the skin on the back of her neck start to prickle.

'Clarke Engineering,' she read. 'All enquiries to Ben Clarke.' There was a familiar logo, along with a phone number and a contact address.

'Is something wrong?' James asked, coming over to her. 'You've gone as white as a sheet.'

She turned to him, and looked at him blankly. All she could see was that business card, emblazoned with her father's name.

'What happened?' he persisted. 'Has something upset you?'

'No, nothing at all,' she told him. 'I'm all right. It's probably just that we've been cooped up in this room for quite a while.' She couldn't tell him what was wrong. He wouldn't understand, would he? James couldn't know that the notice had stirred up memories that she would far rather push to the back of her mind. She didn't fully understand it herself, but seeing the name written there had been enough to bring all the loneliness, heart-ache and sad disillusionment flooding back.

It had never occurred to her that her father would be living nearby. What would she do if she were to run into him one day? She frowned. Perhaps it would never happen. After all, he had stayed away for all these years.

'Is there a problem?'

Amelie looked up to see that Gage had come to join them. He sent a swift glance over her and James, and she gathered her wits about her and shook her head.

'No,' she said quickly. 'Everything's fine. It's hot in here, though, and I think I'd like to go and get some fresh air.'

He looked at her thoughtfully for a moment or two. 'There's a small quadrangle just beyond the doors at the end of the corridor. You could go out there and take a break for a while. You'll not be needed back here for half an hour or so.'

She nodded. 'I'll do that.' Without saying anything more, she turned and walked over to the door.

As she left the room, she glanced back and saw that Gage was looking over the notice-board, frowning as he studied its contents.

She hurried out to the paved square he had described. It was beautiful there, and peaceful. Summer had come to a close, but the weather was still warm, and it was dry out here, so that the air was fresh and reviving. There were flowers set out in tubs dotted about the area, geraniums, petunias and Surfinias, providing great splashes of colour that brightened the place and made it an appealing corner where she could sit and absorb the sun's rays. She went over to a bench seat and sat down, looking to where the branches of trees gave dappled shade.

It was a good place to be, and just sitting there for a few minutes helped to calm her down. How had Gage picked up on the fact that something was wrong? James had been close by, so it was reasonable to expect that he might have noticed anything amiss, but Gage had been across the far side of the room. She didn't know what to make of him. Was he conscious of everything that went on around him?

'I wondered if you would like some coffee. You left yours behind, so I brought you a fresh cup.'

Amelie looked around, and saw that Gage had come to join her in the quadrangle. 'That was thoughtful of you,' she said. 'Thank you.' She accepted the cup from him, and he came and sat beside her on the bench.

'It's tranquil out here, isn't it?' Gage commented. 'I often come out here to take a break when A and E has been particularly frantic. I find it helps me to get my thoughts in order and restores my equilibrium…plus the air is fresh and clean. You somehow end up feeling good about yourself when you've spent a little time out here.'

'Yes, I think I agree with you.' She sipped her coffee and let the hot liquid revive her spirits.

He studied her face momentarily, and then said in a quiet tone, 'I saw that you were looking at the notice-board earlier, and I guess you must have seen the item about our medical equipment supplier…Ben Clarke. It made me wonder…is he a relative of yours?'

She nodded. 'He's my father.'

'I wondered about that. Have you moved back to the area to be close to him? I suppose your medical training must have taken you from one place to another over the years, but perhaps your roots are here?'

'No, in fact, my moving here had nothing to do with my father. My brother lives around here, and that was certainly a factor. I was glad that I managed to lease a cottage that was situated perfectly for me, not too far from where he's living.'

Her brother's friend, Lewis, had found it for her. The cottage next door to his had been without a tenant, and he had brought it to her attention as soon as he'd known that she was coming to the area. Lewis was a good friend and neighbour. She had known him from when her brother had been a teenager, and they had kept in touch over the years. He was always there to lend a hand whenever she needed it.

'And your other reasons for coming here? I recall you mentioned the hospital.'

'Yes, I wanted to be near to where I was going to work, and I chose to come here because this is a renowned teaching hospital. It has a good reputation.'

'That's true enough.' He paused. 'And what about your father? He relocated his business to this area just a few months ago, as I understand it. Was that a coincidence?'

'Probably. At the time, I didn't know that he would be around.'

'So you weren't looking to meet up with him? I get the impression that you're not close—in a family sense?'

She shook her head. 'I haven't seen him in a long time.'

'I'm sorry.'

'Don't be. I'm not.'

He sent her a quizzical look and it occurred to her that his interest in her relationship with her father might be more than just casual. She finished off her coffee and then asked cautiously, 'Do you know him? Have you had dealings with him at all?'

He nodded. 'We put in a big order for equipment, and he came and demonstrated how we should operate it. I found him easy to talk to, and an excellent businessman. He's very astute and clear-sighted about his business interests.'

'Oh, yes,' she said on a dry note. 'He would be. He was always very much driven where his business was concerned.'

'We got along very well. He seems to be a good man, very likable, with a sense of humour and very caring, wanting to do the right thing.'

She raised a finely arched brow. 'Really?'

His eyes narrowed on her. 'You don't sound as though you agree with my view of him.'

Amelie shrugged. 'I'm sure he could sweet-talk his way around anything. You've only had business dealings with him. It's an altogether different matter when you happen to be part of his family. You get used to being sidelined then.'

Gage frowned. 'Do you think you might be misjudging him? I don't mean to be divisive, but after all, most men will put everything they have into their career, so that they can support the family.'

'I think I know my own father. Personally, I wouldn't give him the time of day, but you've obviously built up some kind of rapport with him. It's probably a male bonding type of situation. After all, men stick together, don't they?' Her mouth made a bitter twist.

'That had a biting edge to it.' He studied her curiously. 'Do you have a problem with all men, or just with your father?'

'Let's just say I have reservations, shall we? Once bitten, twice shy, and all that.'

'I see.'

She doubted that, but he didn't press her any more on the subject, and after a short time they made their way back to the meeting. It was only later that it occurred to her that she had been brusque with her new boss, but it was too late to make amends. He had touched a raw wound and suffered the sharp edge of her tongue in response.

If he had entertained any thoughts that his new senior house officer might be sweet and malleable, he was probably rapidly adjusting them right now.

CHAPTER FOUR

'THERE'S a patient waiting for you in the far cubicle,'
Gage said. 'Will you take a look at him and let me know
what you think? And let me see your charts before you
discharge anyone.'

Amelie nodded. 'I will.'

'And make sure that you keep concise notes at all
times. I want you to record any findings on examina-
tion and be sure to list all your investigations.'

'I'll do that.'

'Good. By the way, there'll be a meeting in my office
that I want you to attend later on today…this afternoon,
in fact. I'll get James to cover for you.'

'OK.' She had no idea what that was about, but
perhaps he wanted to go over a few procedural points.
He was keen that everything should be done right, and
he wasn't the sort of person to leave anything to chance.
After working for more than a week in the department,
she was beginning to see how things worked and she
was starting to feel more at home.

Up to now, she had kept a fairly low profile where
Gage was concerned. It bothered her that she had been
slightly caustic with him over his feelings of affinity

with her father, but she wasn't about to take her words back. He hadn't mentioned it since, but she was aware that he was keeping a guarded eye on her.

She went to examine the patient he'd mentioned, a diabetic, and then took a moment to help herself to coffee from the machine in the corridor. James came to join her.

'How's it going?' she asked him. She could see that he looked worried.

'I'm not sure,' he said. 'I'm treating someone for a heart rhythm abnormality, and I'm not quite certain how to proceed. I thought at first there was ventricular fibrillation, but in fact I think it's tachycardia. The electrical axis is constantly changing and I'm a bit out of my depth.'

'Do you want me to come and have a look?'

'Would you?' He sounded relieved. 'I'm a bit reluctant to approach Gage with it just at the moment. He's busy with another patient, and his case is probably more critical than mine.'

'I know how you feel,' Amelie murmured, 'but you shouldn't hesitate to ask if you have a problem, you know. He seems approachable enough.'

'I know, but we're short-staffed, and I heard that he was having trouble getting people to fill in. I think Gage has his work cut out, trying to be in five places at once. He's good with the patients, though. They always seem to come first in his book. I'm just wary of adding to the pressure.'

She smiled. 'Don't be. Isn't that why he's in charge? He's better able to handle it.' She went with him to see the patient and studied the chart that James had made out. 'Have you done blood tests to find out the magnesium level?' she asked.

He nodded. 'I'm still waiting on the results.'

'You'll probably find that's the cause of the trouble. If the magnesium level is too low, that can lead to problems, and then you need to find out why the level was low in the first place.'

'Thanks, Amelie. With you and Chloe helping out, I'm sure I'll get there in the end. I'm not quite on top of things yet. I'm having to retake some exams and I've a lot of extra studying to do, besides being on duty here.'

'I know. It can be difficult when you're new to everything.'

Shortly after that, things started to become even more hectic than usual. People were brought in from a road traffic accident, and Amelie was kept busy treating crush injuries and fractures, and just when she thought she was winning through she found herself dealing with a patient who suddenly went into cardiac arrest.

He was a young boy, about fifteen years old, and Amelie froze momentarily as she saw his condition deteriorate. Then her training surged to the fore and she thumped his chest and felt for a carotid pulse. There wasn't one.

'I need a crash team here,' she called out. 'Cardiac arrest—I need help.'

While she waited for the team to appear, she started mouth-to-mouth respiration and then began chest compressions, pressing down on his chest in order to push blood out of the heart and around the body.

When the team arrived, she quickly put in an airway while the nurse continued with the chest compressions.

'I've put up a central line.' Gage was there by the bedside, and Amelie was reassured by his presence.

'He's in V-fib,' she said. 'I need to shock the heart.' She had to save this boy. How could she live with herself if she didn't pull him through?

Quickly, she placed the paddles on the boy's chest and gave the initial shock.

She glanced at the monitor and saw that her attempt had failed. She tried again and then said, 'I want to try a shot of adrenaline,' before continuing with her attempts to resuscitate the boy.

Gage administered the adrenaline. He hadn't taken over, but had simply let her carry on, and she wondered if that was a deliberate act, because he believed that she could deal with this.

'There's a pulse,' Chloe said, and Amelie gave a sigh of relief.

'Thank heaven.'

'He's doing all right now,' Gage murmured a few minutes later. He was looking at her with that curious, watchful gaze that she was coming to know so well.

'He is, isn't he?' Amelie swallowed, letting the tension seep out of her. 'I was so afraid that he wouldn't make it.'

'He will now, thanks to you.' Gage was smiling at her, and that was something she hadn't seen before. His expression stunned her. The smile lightened his features and did something incredible to his eyes, making them an intense, fascinating grey-blue.

Under that penetrating gaze, her mouth curved in response, and she felt the heat run through her veins, warming her through and through.

He turned away and went back to his patient, but Amelie was glowing inside, and the feeling stayed with her throughout the next hour or so.

'Will you look at this patient's foot for me, when you've a moment?' Chloe asked. 'She was stung by a jellyfish while she was swimming in the sea, and she's in a lot of pain. I have to go and help with a fracture patient, but I don't want to leave her in that state for too long.'

'Yes, of course. Is there any anaphylactic shock?' Amelie asked. 'Any difficulty breathing, or convulsions?'

'Nothing like that, but she's been vomiting.'

Amelie went to examine the woman who had been stung, and was surprised when Gage decided to come along with her. 'I'm going for my lunch-break,' he said, 'but I just wanted to fill you in on the details of this afternoon's meeting. Do you mind if I do it while you're with your patient?'

'Not at all.'

'Good. I just want to go over a few of the issues on patient transfer.'

'All right.'

He ran through some of the items on the agenda as she was examining the woman's foot, and Amelie realised that she already had some ideas about the issues that would come up at the meeting.

She concentrated her attention on her patient. 'It does look nasty,' she commented a few minutes later. 'I'll give you something to relieve the pain, and we'll do what we can to prevent any further damage. Each time the stinging capsules are touched, they release their venom, so we'll start by running vinegar over them to deactivate them.'

Once she had done that, she applied adhesive tape to remove the tentacle fragments, aware that Gage was looking on the whole time. She hoped that she would be able to make the woman feel more comfortable. A large area of the foot was swollen.

'How are you feeling now?' she asked her some time later, when she had done all that she could to ease her pain.

'Much better,' the woman said. 'I didn't realise that these stings could hurt so much.'

Amelie nodded in sympathy.

'I've never experienced one myself,' Gage murmured, 'but you were lucky that it wasn't a Portuguese man-of-war. From what I've heard, they have particularly painful stings. Luckily, we don't come across them very often.'

The woman shuddered. 'I think I'm going to steer clear of swimming in the sea from now on,' she confided.

Amelie left her with a nurse and walked over to the reception desk with Gage. He sent Amelie a swift glance. 'How do *you* feel about the sea now? Do you have any worries about it, after what happened to you?'

Amelie nodded. 'To be honest, I'm trying not to think about it. I used to like going to the beach and watching the waves come in, but now I find it really scary. I think I'd sooner avoid it altogether.'

His dark gaze moved over her. 'I thought you might feel that way. It will take you a while to get over what happened to you.' He glanced at his watch, and said, 'I should go. I have a lunch meeting scheduled with management.'

'Me, too...not with management, but with my brother.' Amelie stayed behind a little longer to write up her notes and file the patient's chart in the tray on the desk. Then she, too, went for lunch.

She and Nathan were meeting up at a local café.

'Amelie,' her brother said, when she walked in. 'I'm glad you could make it. I wasn't sure whether you would be caught up in an emergency of some kind.' He drew her to a table by the window.

'No, it worked out well today. Nathan, it's good to see you.' She gave him a hug and looked at him with affection. His black hair had been recently cut in a short, neat style that suited his square-jawed face, and he looked good, but she knew instantly that something was wrong. Perhaps it was the faint shadowing around his eyes that alerted her, or maybe a slight downward tilt to his mouth that caused her to wonder, but she asked softly, 'Are you all right? You seem a bit troubled.'

They seated themselves and the waitress came and took their order. 'I'm OK, sort of.' There was a tell-tale crease in his brow, and his green eyes were faintly troubled. 'I went in to work this morning and some of the dogs were wandering free in the compound. I don't understand it. I'm sure that I bolted the gate, but I was the last one there last night and it was my job to lock up, so the boss is blaming me. The same thing happened yesterday.'

'That's worrying.' She looked at him intently. 'It's never happened before, has it? Are the animals all right?'

'Yes, luckily, they're fine. There was a lot of mess—damage to some of the feed sacks and water everywhere from where one of the water barrels had been over-turned. I just can't think how it happened. I always make sure I lock up properly.'

'At least they didn't escape from the centre, so no real harm was done. That's the main thing, isn't it?'

'You're right. I dare say the boss will calm down, eventually.' He pressed his lips together in an odd sort of grimace, and Amelie studied him for a moment or two.

'Do you think there will be repercussions?'

'I don't know.' His mouth flattened. 'I need this job. I was looking to go to veterinary college, as you know, and if I could stay on at the centre in a part-time capacity, it will help keep me in funds.'

She laid a hand on his. 'They can't sack you for one misdemeanour, can they? It isn't as though they could prove that it was your fault. Someone else might have been responsible.'

'Maybe.' He was still looking dejected, and Amelie sent him a searching glance.

'Is there something else? Some other problem at work?'

He shook his head. 'Nothing like that... It's just that I had a letter from Dad this morning. He suggested that we might get together some time. He said he had tried to get in touch with you, but he realised that you must have moved house.'

Amelie braced herself a little. 'What are you going to do?'

'I don't know. I just feel this resentment bubbling up inside me. Part of me says that I should ignore the letter, because he does this from time to time, turning up like a bad penny when we least expect him to. But then I started to wonder... I don't see why I should care about him, but another part of me says, He's your father and you should at least make the effort to see him.'

Amelie's mouth made a straight line. 'The same applies to him, doesn't it? He didn't trouble himself about us when we were younger. I feel much the same way that you do. Every now and again, he breezes into our lives and makes us care about him and want to be with him, and then he disappears just as suddenly as he arrived.' She shook her head. 'I don't think I can go through all that again.'

Nathan nodded. 'I thought you might feel that way. I can't make up my mind what to do. I think I'll just leave it a while and think things over. I've enough problems to cope with just now, with Emma and Connor. Emma's all over the place with her emotions and doesn't want us to be together, and the lad gets upset every time I have to leave him.'

'I'm so sorry, Nathan.'

He grimaced. 'It would help if her father would accept me as part of her life, but I doubt that will happen any time soon. Still, we'll work something out, I suppose.'

They ate and talked some more, and Amelie took her leave of him some time later. 'Come over to the cottage as soon as you get the chance,' she said.

'I will. That would be good.'

Amelie hurried back to A and E and made her way to Gage's office in time for the meeting. She had hoped to slide into the room unnoticed, but Gage said quietly, 'Come and take a seat. We were about to make a start.'

She sat where he indicated, next to the specialist registrar, a stylish woman in her early thirties, with blonde hair cut in a silky, smooth bob. There were two other doctors in the room, and when everyone was settled, Gage started the meeting, beginning with some discussion of management issues that didn't directly apply to Amelie.

Her thoughts drifted momentarily. Nathan had talked about his problems with Emma and Connor, and she was anxious about how those relationships were going to work out.

Connor was troubled, he said, and surely that was only going to be resolved when Nathan did something to make the boy a permanent part of his life. As it was, they lived separately, and even though he kept in touch with his son right now, who could tell how long he would go on doing that if Emma was to push him away? Wasn't Nathan turning out to be behaving in much the same way as their father? Could any man be trusted to do the right thing?

'Do you have a viewpoint on that, Amelie?' Gage's deep voice intruded on her thoughts and she looked up and gazed at him blankly.

'Um...sorry... Could you run that by me again?'

His dark eyes narrowed on her. He knew that she had not been listening, and she felt a rush of heat sweep along her cheekbones. 'Gina has just suggested that we need to rethink the procedures regarding patient transfer from this hospital to another. She feels that there can sometimes be problems with equipment failure, bearing in mind that we often have to send medical equipment along with the patient. Have you any ideas as to how we might deal with that?'

Amelie thought about it for a moment or two, and perhaps Gina doubted that she was going to come up with an answer because she said, 'We do have the equipment monitored on a regular basis, of course. It might be that we need to have secondary units on standby.'

Amelie frowned. Wasn't her father's company the one that did the monitoring? Her eyes darkened as she thought about Nathan's reaction to his letter. Why did he have to turn up now, when she was trying to get her life on track and leave the past behind her?

She looked up, and saw that Gage was watching her. Something in his expression told her that he knew what she was thinking. His mouth softened a touch and something kindled in his eyes, as though he would have reached out to her and tried to soothe her angry soul.

Amelie pulled herself together. 'You could be right,' she said, 'though I've found that most equipment failure is due to faulty batteries or low battery life. Not that I've experienced many failures… I just feel that it might be useful to carry a few spares—that would seem to me to be important even on inter-departmental transfers.'

'That sounds like a reasonable suggestion,' Gage murmured. 'I'll make a note of it. Anything else?'

'Not as far as equipment failure goes, but I do have reservations about the documentation that should go along with a patient. I'd prefer a standardised form giving details such as patient's name, birth date, GP, and so on, along with information about management of his condition so far, drugs, responses and the names of the physicians involved.'

'Wouldn't that be a bit long-winded?' another doctor asked. 'If we're trying to hurry things along, we don't want to be filling in extra forms, do we?'

Amelie grimaced. 'Maybe not, but it doesn't have to take more than a minute or two to fill in the details, and someone could be allocated to do that while the patient is being made ready. A standard form would help clarify thinking and the receiving doctor would have all the information to hand. I think it would be extremely useful.'

He appeared to contemplate the idea. 'You may be

right,' he murmured. 'You know, the biggest problem I find is arranging the transfer in the first place. When I think of the hours spent chasing up bed space, it's enough to make you tear your hair out... And then you could finish up having to send someone to a hospital that's miles away.'

'That's true, it can be a nightmare,' Gage remarked, 'and the last thing you want is for your very sick patient to be travelling over long distances.'

The meeting broke up a short time after that, but the registrar stayed behind to go over some paperwork with Gage, and Amelie wandered out into the corridor with the other two doctors. Her mind was still fixed on the deliberations of the last half-hour, and more especially on Gage's unspoken response to her troubled thoughts. She didn't have time to dwell on things for long, though.

'Do you have a moment?' Chloe asked, coming to find her. 'There's someone in cubicle four that you might want to look at... I think he's a friend of yours. He brought your belongings in for you when you were a patient here the other day. His name's Lewis Wake-field.'

Amelie was startled. Nathan's friend was here? 'Are you saying that he's here as a patient? What's wrong with him?'

'He says that he was injured at work, at the animal rescue centre—it's a dog bite. He asked if you would see to him if you were free, and I said I thought that would be all right.'

'Yes, of course I'll go and see him.' A dog bite? Lewis was wonderful with animals. He worked with them every day, so why on earth would one of them attack him?

She hurried over to the cubicle. The curtains were open, and she saw her neighbour sitting on the chair in there. His brown hair fell in a light wave across his forehead, obscuring his features, but when he looked up she saw that his face was streaked with blood.

'Lewis,' she said, shocked. 'I can't believe that I'm seeing this. How did it happen?' His face was a mess. His lip was swollen and cut, and she could see that his arm hadn't escaped either. There was a ring of tooth marks on his forearm and the bruising was already becoming apparent.

'It wasn't the dog's fault,' he said quickly. 'She was jittery to begin with because things have been a bit upset around the place lately. I expect Nathan told you about that. She had pups a few weeks ago, and I think she was protecting them. There was a lot of noise and commotion and I don't think she realised it was me coming towards her.'

'What kind of dog is she?'

'She's not a pedigree. She's more golden retriever than anything else…it's not usually a ferocious breed.'

'I remember now. I saw her when I came to the centre one time. Her pups are gorgeous.' Amelie took a closer look at the wound. 'Even so, she's made a mess of your face. That lip is going to need stitches.' She touched his shoulder lightly in a gesture of sympathy.

'She was probably alarmed by things that have been going on. We're not sure if someone is breaking in at night after we've all gone home, and a lot of the animals are edgy. The gate was undone again this morning when I arrived at work and there was chaos everywhere, with the dogs roaming the compound.'

Amelie grimaced. 'Is Nathan in much trouble over this?'

'Well, it doesn't look too good for him. It's his turn to lock up throughout this week, but this is the second time the bolts haven't been secured. I just can't see Nathan forgetting to do it. He might have been a bit out of sorts these last few days, but he's always been reliable up to now.'

'I know.' She was uneasy, though. Was her brother under pressure of some kind? Was his relationship with Emma beginning to affect the way he carried out his responsibilities at work? Or could it be that he was concerned about the letter he had received from their father?

'Is everything all right in here?' Gage came into the cubicle, and looked from one to the other. He glanced to where Amelie's fingers rested on Lewis's shoulder, and she let her hand drop to her side. It wouldn't do to have Gage thinking that she was being too familiar with a patient.

'Yes, everything's under control…but I think he'll need to see a maxillofacial specialist,' she said. 'I wouldn't want to try to suture this. It needs an expert touch.'

He moved in to take a closer look. 'You're right. You'll need to get someone down here to look at him.' He inspected Lewis's arm. 'That one isn't so serious. The skin is broken in places and you'll have quite a bit of bruising there, but there's no major damage. It will just need cleaning, and a dressing.'

He studied Lewis. 'What will happen to the dog that did this to you? Was it a family pet?'

'No. It was one of the dogs at the animal rescue centre, where I work. Nothing will happen to her. It isn't our policy to put the dogs to sleep and, anyway, I don't believe that she meant to harm me. She acted defensively, I'm sure, but the long and the short of it is, she caught me as I was bending to see to one of her pups.' He turned to look at Amelie. 'You know, there's one that was the smallest of the litter, and we've had to take special care of him to see him through. Do you remember Rags?'

She nodded. 'I do. He was a pathetic little thing.'

'At one time we thought we might lose him, but he's doing well now.' He smiled. 'I had it in mind that Connor might like to have him. He loves dogs, doesn't he?'

Amelie nodded. 'I don't know about him having a puppy, though. They take a lot of looking after, and he would need the run of the garden, wouldn't he?'

Gage sucked in a sharp breath and suddenly straightened, as though a thought had occurred to him. He slanted Lewis a penetrating gaze. 'You were in here the other day, weren't you, to see Amelie, when she was in Recovery?'

'That's right. I brought her clothes in for her.'

'Yes, I remember now.' Gage was frowning. He started to move away from the bedside. 'I should go and see to my other patients, so I'll leave you in Amelie's capable hands,' he said, his tone brisk. 'I'm sure the surgeon will make a good job of your sutures. He's very skilled at what he does.'

He turned to Amelie, and said shortly, 'I'll leave you to finish up in here.'

She nodded. It seemed to her that his mood had changed, but she couldn't fathom in what way. She stared up at him. His features were partly in shadow, but his expression had taken on a faintly austere appearance and she wondered if he was going to say something more, but he didn't. He simply turned and walked out of the cubicle.

She didn't quite know what to make of it. Had he made some sort of connection between her and Lewis and Connor? Surely he wasn't putting two and two together and making five? And why would that bother him, anyway?

Instead of spending any more time trying to work out what had just happened, she turned her attention back to Lewis. 'I'll need to give you an anti-tetanus injection,' she told him, 'and I'll prescribe some antibiotics to prevent any chance of infection. The nurse will come in to clean up the wounds for you.'

'Thanks, Amelie.' He glanced at her thoughtfully. 'Your boss is an unusual sort of fellow, isn't he? It's hard to make out what's going on in his head. Do you and he get on?'

'He's all right. They think a lot of him around here. He's a very well-respected consultant.'

His gaze was watchful. 'That's not what I asked.'

Amelie made a wry face. 'The truth is, Lewis, we get on all right, but I'm reserving judgement on him. I'm still getting to know him.'

He tipped his head to one side and studied her. 'That might take some time, knowing the way you are. You're very wary of letting your guard down around men, aren't you? I've noticed that in you before. Is that because of your background? I know that you and Nathan both felt let down when your father left the family home. I suppose that must have had an ongoing effect on you.'

'Maybe. My father was a love-them-and-leave-them kind of man, and it didn't seem to matter whether it was his family or other women that he was leaving. He was always ready to move on to something or someone new. I don't think I'm going to willingly lay myself open to that kind of hurt.'

'Do you want to talk to me about it?'

She shook her head. 'No, I don't think I do.' She had known Lewis for a long time—since they'd been teenagers—but she felt uncomfortable laying open her soul this way.

'OK.' He put up his hands to show that he was backing off. 'I know it's a sore point, so I won't ask any more. At least, not for a while, anyway.' He grinned.

'Good.' She was thankful that he had given in. Lewis was like that, though, good-natured, a true friend, someone that she could rely on in a crisis.

'The nurse will come and clean the wounds up for you,' she told him, 'and I'll chase up the specialist for you, but I'll have to leave you for a while, I'm afraid. I really need to go and look after my other patients. I promise, though, I'll try my best to come and see you before you go.'

'Thanks, Amelie. Thanks for looking in on me.'

'Any time.'

She went back to work, but her mind was all over the place. What was she to make of Gage? He seemed to blow hot and cold, and she didn't understand him at all. Was it simply pressure of work, or was something wrong?

He caught up with her again an hour or so later as she was writing up some lab forms at the desk. 'You haven't signed off on your diabetes patient yet,' he said, his tone brisk. 'Weren't you supposed to be sending him to the intensive therapy unit? What's causing the delay?'

'I'm still waiting on the results of some tests.'

He frowned. 'You can send them through as soon as you get them.'

'I know, but there isn't a bed available just yet anyway. I'm still trying to sort it out.'

'OK.' He inclined his head briefly. 'If you have any problem with that, let me know. Remember, we need to keep things moving in here. I don't want any log jams building up.'

With that, he walked away in search of his next patient, and Amelie watched him and wondered why she was left feeling so out of sorts. What did it matter to her that his manner was terse?

She finished writing up the lab forms and went to check up on her remaining patients. She was on edge, and it was all because of Gage's manner towards her, wasn't it? He had a way of unsettling her, of making her far more aware of him than she was comfortable with. She didn't want to start caring about him, or wonder what he was thinking, especially when she had to work with him.

CHAPTER FIVE

'ARE you taking me to school today?' Connor said, looking at Amelie across the breakfast table. 'Daddy made me late when he took me, and the teacher was cross. She said we're supposed to get there before the register.'

'Did she? Oh, dear.' Amelie frowned. 'Well, we'll have to see if we can do any better than that, won't we? Yes, I'm taking you there today, because your dad had to go in to work early.'

He frowned. 'When's my mummy's coming home?'

'In a few days. She needs to stay with Grandma at the holiday cottage until your grandma's feeling a bit better.'

He seemed to accept that explanation happily enough and turned his attention back to his food. Amelie sent him a rueful, affectionate look. Was there any way at all that she could speed this morning's activities up a little? It seemed doubtful. He was still munching on toast, and the jam had smeared on to his T-shirt, which meant she would have to whip that off him and find another for him to put on if he was to look respectable at school. She sighed. Her washing pile was growing by the minute and Connor had only been with her for a day or so.

'Why has Daddy gone to work early? Is he in trouble?'

'No, he isn't in trouble,' she told him, 'but he wants to go in and see how the animals are doing, and perhaps he might need to clear up a few spills before the boss gets there.'

'That's because the dogs keep getting out and knocking things over,' Connor said knowledgeably. 'Daddy says he doesn't know why it's happening. He locks up, but the dogs still get out.' He rolled his eyes. 'He says he must be going out of his mind.' He used an exaggerated tone and clapped a hand to his head as though he was imitating his father's actions. Then he stared at her questioningly. 'Is he going out of his mind?'

Amelie laughed. 'No, Connor. Your dad will be fine. Don't you worry about that. Just eat up and let's get out to the car, or I shall be late and *my* boss will be the one who starts getting cross.'

Some half an hour later, she finally managed to get Connor into the car, and they set off for the nursery school. He hurried into his classroom happily enough and, after giving him a hug and a kiss, she waved him off. Then she made her way to the hospital.

Ever since Nathan had asked if Connor could stay over at her place for a few days, things had been chaotic. She didn't mind, because she understood that Emma needed to be with her mother, but she wasn't used to having a small child stay with her overnight. It couldn't be helped, though. Nathan's flat was being renovated, and there was plaster dust everywhere, so it really wouldn't have been a good idea for the child to stay there.

Hurrying into A and E, she grabbed her white coat from the locker room and shrugged into it. She had only just made it in to work on time, and her mind was still racing from the morning rush. Smoothing down her skirt and turning around, a minute or two later, she almost collided with Gage, and she gave a little start of surprise. 'Oh... I didn't see you there.'

'I gathered that.' He sent her a considering look. 'Are you all right? You look a bit hassled. Are you still having problems getting in to work?'

She grimaced. 'It's only a temporary glitch. I really don't think it will happen again.' She flicked him a quick glance as she pushed her stethoscope into her pocket. 'It's just that everything seems to take twice as long as it should. Connor doesn't really know the meaning of "Let's hurry up, shall we?"' She tried a smile. 'I'll be better organised tomorrow, I hope.'

He looked at her curiously. 'Are you still having to cope with all this on your own? Chloe told me that you live alone...you don't share your house with anyone. It came up when you were brought in as a patient and we needed to put your details on the file.'

'Yes, that's right, I do.'

'Isn't there anyone who could help out...grandparents, perhaps? There are grandparents, aren't there?'

She shook her head. 'Not really. You know about the situation with my dad, and my mother isn't with us any more. His other grandmother isn't well, and his grandad can only really help out for short periods of time. He loves him to bits, but he isn't up to looking after a small boy for any great length of time.'

Gage winced. 'That's unfortunate.' They started to walk back towards the main area of A and E. 'It's a good thing that you're so resilient,' he murmured. 'You're only just out of hospital, and now you have a tough, demanding job here in A and E, as well as having to cope with a young child. It can't be easy for you.'

She was surprised and touched by his interest and his expression of concern. 'I'll get by,' she murmured. 'Sometimes you don't have very much choice in these things.'

'Maybe, but you must let me know if things get too much for you.'

'Thank you.' Her gaze lingered on him for a while, but he was already starting to turn away towards the desk, his mind on other things.

He was kind and supportive, and she was beginning to realise that he was a man she could respect, a man she could turn to in times of trouble. He was not at all what she had expected when she had first come there.

When she had applied for this posting, she had heard all sorts of rumours about the consultant in charge, and how exacting he could be. It hadn't put her off. This was where she wanted to be, and she was determined to make a success of working in A and E. She guessed that Gage was probably the best person to help her to do that.

He was very young to have reached his position, still only in his mid-thirties, but he was a go-getter, someone who'd risen very fast in his profession, and people said that he had achieved it all through merit. He was a brilliant physician, and he was constantly striving to update his skills.

Amelie went to look through the patients' files. The specialist registrar was already at the desk, checking her notes. 'Gage,' Gina said, 'I'm glad that I've caught up with you. I'd appreciate a second opinion on one of my patients.'

'Of course. What's wrong?'

'The patient's complaining of a really bad headache, and there's a low-grade fever, as well as altered vision. I'm not absolutely sure about the diagnosis, but I was thinking that perhaps it was temporal arteritis. Would you mind coming and taking a look at him with me?'

'I'd be glad to.' They walked away, an easy familiarity between them.

Amelie turned away from the desk and went to find her first patient of the day. From then on, she was kept so busy that she didn't see much of Gage until late in the afternoon, when he came to advise James on a patient.

'Do you think I should get a surgeon down here?' James asked. 'My patient is nineteen years old and complaining of pain in his neck after a fall. There are some neurological signs and his symptoms seem to be getting worse. I've done an X-ray, but it's quite difficult to interpret. I might be worrying about nothing, but at the same time I don't want to risk sending the man home if it's possible that he has a broken neck.'

'Let me take a look,' Gage said. 'It's always wise to err on the side of caution if you're not sure about something. Where do you think the problem might be, specifically?'

'I'm worried in case I'm missing a fracture of the odontoid peg.'

Gage studied the X-rays with him, and after a moment or two he said quietly, 'It's difficult to see, but I think you may be right to be concerned.' He turned to Amelie. 'Come and take a look. See what you think.'

Amelie was glad to be included on the exercise. She respected Gage's skill as a doctor, and any chance to learn how to interpret difficult X-ray films was a bonus. She went to check them in the light-box. 'It's very hard to make out anything at all.' She pointed to a faint line on the film. 'Is that it?'

Gage nodded. 'It certainly does look as though there's a break in the bone.' He turned to look at James. 'You did well to spot that. I would get a surgeon down here to come and examine him. If he agrees with the diagnosis, your patient will need traction and a halo jacket with posterior fusion.'

James winced. 'Thanks. I'll go and deal with it right away.' He hurried off to do that.

Gage was still studying the films when Amelie went back to the desk. 'I need to get these blood samples sent off to the lab,' she told Chloe, who was busy checking notes on the computer.

'Leave them with me. I'll get the porter to take them for you,' the nurse murmured. 'He has to go that way.' She glanced up at Amelie. 'Actually, I was just about to come looking for you. There was a phone call for you just a few minutes ago, but something happened and it was cut off. I checked up and wrote down the number for you.'

'Thanks.' Amelie looked at the number Chloe had written on the notepad, and saw that it was Nathan's mobile. 'It was my brother,' she told her. 'I'd better go and find out what it was that he wanted.'

Nathan was supposed to be collecting Connor from nursery school, and if there was a problem that prevented him from doing that, she would have to make other arrangements.

She dialled his mobile and let it ring for some time. Eventually, just as she was about to give up on him, he answered, and she was shocked by the sound of his voice. 'Amelie,' he said in a gasping tone, 'I need... help...' There was a clatter, as though he had dropped the phone, and then the line went dead.

'Is something wrong?' Gage said, coming to stand beside her. 'You look worried.'

'I think my brother's in trouble,' she told him. 'We were cut off, but from what I heard it sounds as though something's badly wrong.'

Chloe gave her a look of friendly concern. 'What are you going to do?'

Amelie frowned. 'I think I'll ring his workplace first of all and see if they know anything about what's going on.'

She went away to do that and came back to them a few minutes later. 'He isn't there,' she told Gage, 'and his boss has no idea where he could be. He sent him out to get medication for the animals from the local vet hours ago, and he hasn't returned yet. The vet hasn't seen anything of him either.' She glanced at her watch. 'I really need to know what's happened to him. He sounded terrible on the phone.'

'Do you think he's ill?'

'It's possible. I thought he was feeling a bit down because of his troubles at work and so on, but it might have been that he was off-colour in some way and I didn't realise it. Just now he sounded very much as though he was in pain.'

'Then you should go,' Gage said, 'if that's what you want to do. There's not too long to the end of your shift, and I'm sure James will be able to cover for you.' He paused, and then added, 'In fact, I should have gone off duty an hour ago, so I could go along with you if you like. It sounds as though you might need some help finding him.'

'Are you sure?' Her brow creased. 'I wouldn't want to put you to any bother. It's my problem after all, and I may have got things wrong. He might be perfectly all right.'

Gage's expression was thoughtful. 'I want to help in any way I can and, besides, I think you've probably had enough to cope with on your own of late. It might be good for you to have someone with you.'

'Thank you.' She sent him a grateful glance. 'I'll most likely be feeling very foolish about all this later on, but I do appreciate you offering to come with me.'

She hadn't realised, until now, how tense she was feeling, but it was actually a relief, knowing that Gage would be with her. It wasn't something she had contemplated, but it gave her a boost of confidence, knowing that he would be there by her side to lend his support. He was strong and capable, and she felt that she could rely on him to know what to do if there was a problem.

'I suppose you've already made arrangements for your boy to be picked up from school?' he queried, as they left the hospital a short time later.

'Connor? Yes, his grandad's going to take care of him until I get home.' She had phoned and made the arrangements as soon as she had realised there might be a problem. It wasn't like Nathan to let the child down, and that was what made her think there was something terribly wrong.

'That's good. Shall we go together in my car? It might be quicker that way, and I can always bring you back here to pick up your car later.'

She nodded. 'OK. I thought we should head for his

workplace first of all, in case he has turned up there, or they know something more. At the least it's a starting point and we can trace his steps from there to the vet's surgery.'

'Whatever you think best.' They walked out to his parking place and he opened the passenger door of his car for her. It was a gleaming silver model, sleek and impressive, and luxurious inside, but Amelie was too keyed up to be able to relax and enjoy it. She was too preoccupied with her worries over Nathan to want to say very much, and she leaned back in her seat and tried to focus her attention on where they were going.

Gage was a competent driver. He covered the miles swiftly, smoothly, so that the journey seemed to take no time at all.

'You live on the back lane by the farm, don't you?' he said, as they drew closer to the rescue centre. 'That's not too far from my place. I'm just a couple of miles from you, in a house overlooking the bay. You've perhaps passed by it on your way in to work if you take the coast road sometimes. You would have seen it from a distance.'

She sensed that he was trying to ease her nerves with conversation. She nodded. 'It's possible. You'll have to point it out to me.'

When they arrived at her brother's workplace, the boss came out to meet them. 'He isn't here,' he said, 'and there still hasn't been any word from him. It's really strange, but he's been a bit odd lately, sort of quiet and withdrawn. We haven't been able to get to the bottom of what was wrong.'

Amelie frowned. 'I know that he's worried about the animals getting out. He's convinced that he had locked up properly each night, and he checked all the bolts. He can't understand what's been happening.'

The man gave an awkward shrug of his shoulders. 'It's true he felt bad about it, but there was something more than that, I think. We didn't know what to make of it, and we wondered if he'd had enough and decided to just walk out.'

Amelie frowned. She couldn't imagine her brother doing something like that. 'Perhaps we'll be able to get to the bottom of it.' She turned back to Gage. 'Shall we go? I'm not sure where Nathan might be, but we could try following the route to the vet's surgery. There might be one or two places where he could have stopped on the way and we could check them out.'

'That sounds reasonable to me.'

They went back to the car and Gage started up the engine once more. 'I didn't see Lewis anywhere around,' he said. 'I'd have thought he would have some idea of what was going on, if he works with your brother. He seemed to me to be a shrewd man.' He slanted her a quick glance. 'Would he have been walking the dogs, or something like that? I saw plenty of other workers around.' He turned the car out on to the main road.

'He's away on a course...similar to the one that Nathan took a while back.'

'Oh, I see. That explains it.' He paused momentarily, and then murmured, 'You and Lewis are very close, aren't you?' He sent her a quick, searching look.

She nodded. 'Yes, we are.'

Amelie was puzzled by that intent look, but then he frowned and added, 'And he certainly appears to be very fond of Connor. He was really keen for him to have one of the pups, wasn't he?'

She smiled. 'He knows how much Connor loves them. He's been to the rescue centre a few times and he fell in love with all the puppies, but with Rags especially.'

Gage was silent for a moment or two and appeared to be giving his attention to the road. She wondered if she ought to say something to him, to clarify her relationship with Lewis, and explain to him that Connor was her nephew, but he broke into her thoughts, saying, 'So, even though he works with him, Lewis hasn't given you any idea of what might be troubling your brother, apart from the animals getting out?'

She shook her head. She probably had it all wrong about his view of Lewis and Connor, and she dismissed the thought to the back of her mind, staring out of the window, looking along the streets for any sign of her brother. She didn't see him. 'There was one thing that troubled him... Nathan had a letter from my father recently, asking if he could meet up with us.'

'Really? How did he react to that?'

'Not very well. It stirred a lot of things up that he would rather have forgotten.' Her mouth straightened. 'You might get on well with my father, but we see an entirely different side of him. He left home when I was nine years old, and my brother was seven. I don't think Nathan ever got over it. He idolised his dad, and his world simply crashed when he left. He kept asking when he was coming back to us.'

'Did he come back?'

'Occasionally. Just when we were getting used to life without him, he would turn up again and we would begin to think that perhaps he was going to stay with us this time.' She grimaced. 'Then he would take off without warning and we went through the whole process of being abandoned yet again. It was painful, for us and for our mother.'

'I can imagine it would be.' His eyes were dark with sympathy. 'You said that Nathan never got over it, but it must have affected you both quite badly.'

'That's true, but I think it was worse for Nathan. He needed a father figure, and he was like a lost soul for a long time. He resented the fact that he had been left behind. He said it was almost as though he had been discarded because he wasn't good enough, and no matter how my mother tried to reassure him he couldn't accept what had happened. He started to act up, and he turned into a rebellious teenager, always in trouble of some sort. I think that's why his girlfriend's parents…or Emma's father, at least…have reservations about him. They believe he's still that same antisocial creature that he was then.'

'But you think he's changed?'

'I do… I did. To be honest, I don't really know any more. He's having these problems at work and he can't seem to get things right with Emma.'

'Nathan obviously needed to have his father around, and being abandoned has probably had a lasting effect on him. Do you think the same applies to Connor? Doesn't he need to have his father there as an integral part of his life?'

Amelie's brows drew together. It was something she had often wondered about. 'I suppose he must be affected by the way things are,' she said, 'but things don't always work out for the best, do they? It's sad, heartbreaking even, but people don't always do the right thing. Couples break up, or things go wrong and they simply don't get together properly in the first place.'

He was giving her that look again, that same intense, questioning gaze. 'How do you feel about it...about the whole business of marriage and the family unit?'

She mulled that over. Was it possible for any relationship to be perfect? She thought about her brother's on-off situation with his girlfriend, and his responsibilities towards his son. Wasn't he following the pattern set by their father? She loved her brother, but she saw what was going on and it made her even more wary of ever wanting to put her trust in a man. How could she do that, when even the men in her own family showed no sign of making a commitment to the women in their lives?

She said slowly, 'I think I would find it hard to relate to any man who didn't show me that he was going to be there for me when it counted. Children need stability, it's true, but you can't always guarantee it.'

'No, you can't.' Gage sent a swift glance over her tense features. 'So you've never been tempted to marry?'

'No, I haven't.'

Perhaps he thought better of probing any further. He peered out of the car window, and murmured, 'There's been no sign of your brother up to now, has there?'

She shook her head.

He slowed the car and lightly drummed his fingers on the steering-wheel. 'I'll park and we can trace the rest of the way on foot. As you said, he might have gone off track for a while, or decided to stop off somewhere on the way, and then perhaps he was taken ill. We'll have a better chance of finding him if we take a closer look at some of the by-ways.'

'I think you're right. He might have decided to sit for a while and think things through.' She frowned. 'I suppose we could try the local park. It's just along the road here.'

Amelie led the way, glancing about her as she walked towards the park gates. She tried her phone again, dialling Nathan's number, but there was no answer. The park was small, with a stretch of beautifully mown grass and a copse of trees to provide shade from the autumn sunshine. A shallow stream meandered through its length, and there were banks of flowers bordering a children's play area. They started the search by a covered seating area.

'He isn't here,' Gage said, after a while, when they had explored every part of the terrain. He put an arm around her shoulders in a gesture of comfort and she welcomed his nearness, the way he was holding her as though he would keep her close and soothe her troubles away. 'I suggest we walk over to the vet's surgery and look around there. If he set off to go on an errand, there's a good chance he might still end up making his way there, if he's able.'

'All right.'

They arrived at the vet's building just a few minutes later. It was an imposing old house, set in its own land-scaped grounds, and Gage went to Reception and asked if they could look around.

The receptionist nodded. 'That's all right. He cer-tainly hasn't come in here, but you're welcome to look around the grounds for him. There's a big car-parking area at the back, and we look out onto fields from there.' She paused. 'I'm not sure where to suggest you search... Sometimes people walk their dogs along by the fence before they bring them in here, or they stop to look over the gate at the horses on the pasture. There's a bit of a picnic area, too, where the staff go sometimes to eat lunch on sunny days. It's around by the outhouses.'

'Thanks.'

Amelie swallowed her disappointment. She had hoped that Nathan would have turned up by now, but there was still no sign of him and she followed Gage outside to the parking area.

'There's no one here,' she said, glancing around, 'except for a man walking his Labrador.'

Gage nodded cautiously. 'But the dog seems a bit distracted, doesn't he? Do you see how his owner is having to draw him back to heel? I wonder if something has caught his attention.'

Amelie would probably not have taken much notice of the man and the dog, but Gage was already striding towards a group of outbuildings that stood to one side of the car park. 'There are some bench seats out here,' he called back to her, 'and tables. This is probably where the staff come and sit to have their lunch.'

Amelie followed him over there. Glancing around, she said, 'I don't see anyone, do you?'

Gage didn't answer. He was looking towards the shrub garden. He suddenly stiffened, and she went towards him to see what it was that had caught his attention.

'I think we might have found your brother, Amelie,' he said quietly. He walked over to a seat that was partially hidden from view by the shrubbery and she saw him go down on to his knees. Hurrying to his side, she pulled in a swift breath when she saw that someone was lying on the ground.

'Nathan?'

Nathan mumbled a reply, but she couldn't tell what he was saying. Gage was already examining him, taking his pulse, checking his responses.

'What's happened to him?' She sank down beside her brother.

'I don't know, but he's in a bad way. His heart rate is galloping and he seems to have a temperature. My guess is that he's in a lot of pain. You stay with him and call for an ambulance while I go back to the car and get my medical bag.'

Amelie dialled the number, and then looked into Nathan's eyes. 'Can you tell me what happened?' she asked him. 'Are you in pain?'

He nodded. 'Didn't…fetch Connor,' he managed.

'I know, it's all right. He's with his grandad.' He let out a short gasp of relief. 'Tell me where you're hurting,' she asked him. 'Can you show me?'

'Thought it would…pass,' he said in a thready voice. She could barely make out what he was saying, but he moved his hand over his abdomen.

'Is that where the pain is?' Her brother was pale, and there was a sheen of sweat on his forehead.

He nodded again. 'Wanted…to rest…for a minute,' he said, 'but it…got worse. I feel sick.'

Gage was back by now and he hunkered down beside Nathan.

'He says he has pain in his abdomen,' Amelie said, 'and it appears to be in the right lower quadrant.' She glanced around. 'From the looks of things, he's been vomiting, but I don't think this is a straightforward stomach bug. He looks as though he's going into shock.'

'You're right.' Gage finished taking his blood pressure. 'His BP is low and he looks as though he's dehydrated. I'm going to put in an intravenous line and we'll give him fluids. Do you want to give him something for the pain while I do that? There's a syringe in my medical bag.'

She nodded, and hurried to give her brother an opioid painkiller. It was frightening to see him looking so ill. 'This should help you to feel a little better,' she told him.

By the time the ambulance arrived, they had done all they could for Nathan for the time being.

'I think he must have tried to ring us,' the driver said. 'The service had a call that was cut off and we were trying to trace where it came from.'

Amelie supervised her Nathan's transfer to the ambulance, and climbed in there to sit beside her brother.

'I'll follow in my car and meet you at the hospital,' Gage told her, and then the paramedic closed the doors on them and the driver started the engine.

'We'll be there in a few minutes,' she told her brother. 'Hang in there.' He looked terrible. His face was ashen and he was barely able to speak, and she worried about how long he had been lying out there on the ground. She wished that Gage was with her. Somehow, things didn't seem quite so bad when he was around.

Amelie found that he was waiting for her, though, as he had promised, when they drew up at the ambulance bay outside A and E a short time later.

'How's he doing?' he asked.

'The pain has eased off a little, but things don't look good.' Amelie watched as the paramedics wheeled Nathan into the emergency room and she felt as though her heart was being squeezed. This was her kid brother, whom she had protected and watched over all their young lives, and she couldn't bear to see him hurting this way. What was happening to him?

'The team are prepared for him,' Gage said, coming to put an arm around her shoulders. 'You know the procedure. They'll do a scan and urinalysis, and blood tests. We should know before too long what's wrong with him.'

'I want to go with him,' she said.

'I know you do, but it's best if you leave the team to deal with him. You're too close and you'll not be able to keep a clear head.' He paused. 'Let's get you inside. We'll go and wait in one of the relatives' rooms.'

He indicated to a nurse where they were going and then ushered Amelie into a side room and closed the door.

'I feel as though I let him down,' she said, pacing the floor. 'Everyone thought that he was behaving oddly, that he wasn't doing his job properly, and even I had my doubts about him. Now it turns out that all the time he must have been ill. I should have seen it. I should have known.' She looked at Gage and blinked away the sting of tears that threatened her eyes. 'Finding him like that, so helpless, in so much pain…it was such a shock.'

He came and stood in front of her, placing his palms on her shoulders and stopping her from pacing. 'You believed in him,' he said. 'You wouldn't be human if you didn't have doubts, but you didn't give up on him. You went looking for him, and you have nothing to feel guilty about.'

He gripped her shoulders gently, and she felt the warmth of his hands seep into her and permeate her whole body. 'Amelie, you saved him. If you hadn't decided to go after him he could have lain there all night. You shouldn't blame yourself for anything.'

She looked up at him. 'I don't know how I would have coped without you. Thank you for coming with me to look for him. It was such a comfort, knowing that you were there, and you were so good at taking care of him. I just couldn't bear it if anything were to happen to Nathan.'

'You mustn't think like that,' he said, folding his arms around her and drawing her to him. 'He's going to come through this…you have to believe that. He's in good hands.'

'I know.' She tried to cling onto that thought. 'I just can't help worrying about him.'

He curved his hand and lifted it to tilt her chin with his forefinger. 'Believe what I'm telling you. You're strong. You'll get through this, and so will he.'

Somehow she must have moved closer to him, because she felt his body warm and strong against hers and she was thankful for it. More than anything, she needed this closeness, this comfort, this feeling that he was there for her.

His glance moved over her, his grey-blue eyes darkening as her gaze meshed with his and her lips seemed to soften. He was still for a moment, hesitating for a second or two. Then he bent his head to her and pressed a gentle kiss to her lips.

Her whole body stirred, a shock wave of electricity flowing through her. That brief touch of his mouth on hers made her forget everything for a moment, so that she was floating somewhere away from all her worries, lost on a blissful cloud of ignorance.

Slowly, reluctantly, he eased back from her, and she stared up at him, her mouth tingling with sweet sensation, heat rippling along her nerve endings, but uncertainty was already welling up inside her. What was she thinking of? Her whole being hungered for him to hold her close, while all the time her head was urging caution.

She was bemused, not knowing why it had come to an end, her mind reeling with the enormity of everything that was happening.

'Someone's coming,' he said softly, as though in explanation. 'It could be news about your brother.'

She turned, watching as the door opened and a nurse came in. 'I thought you might like some coffee,' the girl said, walking over to a table in a corner of the room and placing a tray on it. 'Waiting can be difficult, and a hot drink usually helps to calm the nerves.'

'Thank you.' Amelie pulled in a deep breath, getting herself together. 'Is there any news?'

The nurse shook her head. 'Not yet, I'm afraid. The doctors are still doing tests.'

She went back to the door and left the room, adding, 'Just shout if you want anything. I'll be just around the corner at the nurses' station.'

'Thanks.' Gage nodded, and then went over to the table. Picking up a cup, he handed it to Amelie. 'She's right,' he said. 'Drink that and you'll start to feel better.'

He was calm and utterly in control of himself, distant almost, and Amelie began to ask herself what had just happened between them. Had she imagined that sudden burgeoning of feeling that had exploded inside her?

To give herself time to recover, she did as he suggested and sipped the hot liquid slowly. 'I should ring Connor's grandad and tell him what's happening,' she said.

'Yes, of course.' His gaze was watchful. 'Will he mind looking after Connor for a little while longer, do you think?'

She shook her head. 'I doubt it. It's getting close to Connor's bedtime. I expect he'll sit him down on the settee and Connor will fall asleep before long, if he's warm and cosy.'

They were making small talk, but she sensed that the atmosphere was somehow strained between them now. Was he, too, regretting the kiss?

Gage had simply meant to offer her comfort, nothing more, and she ought to know that she couldn't rely on her instincts to tell her how to go on. It wouldn't do to let her feelings run riot, to let herself care too much for him, would it? If she gave in to her emotions, she would surely end up being hurt.

CHAPTER SIX

'I'M AFRAID I have to tell you that your brother is very ill, Dr Clarke.' The surgeon was an older man, experienced and gentle in his approach, but he was frowning as he spoke and Amelie was filled with apprehension. 'It was fortunate that you and Gage found him when you did, because otherwise I don't believe he would have lasted the night.'

He glanced at Gage. 'The initial treatment you gave him probably helped to save his life. He couldn't have been in better hands.'

'I guessed that he might be suffering from appendicitis,' Gage murmured. 'I just wasn't sure how far things had gone, or whether we had caught it before the appendix perforated, but he looked as though he was in trouble.'

'How did the operation go? Has he come through it all right?' Even as she asked the question, Amelie felt the blood draining from her face, and Gage must have been aware of how wretched she was feeling because he slid an arm around her waist, letting it rest there as though to steady her. He wanted her to know that she was not alone in this, and the gesture gave her a good deal of solace, but nothing could take away her fear for her brother.

The surgeon nodded. 'He has. I've removed the appendix, but he isn't out of the woods yet, by long way. Unfortunately, it had ruptured, causing an infection of the lining of the abdominal cavity. It has resulted in a generalised peritonitis, causing a gram-negative septicaemia.' He was grim-faced. 'I'm sure that you know how serious that can be.'

Amelie nodded. As a doctor, she knew the prognosis all too well. It meant that her brother was going through a life-threatening situation, and if the toxins that were rampaging through his body managed to overwhelm him, he wouldn't survive.

'What are his chances? Do you know?'

He shook his head. 'It's too soon to say. We've performed a peritoneal lavage, and I've put peritoneal drains in position. Of course, we will be monitoring his condition very carefully. The lab results have come back, and we're doing what we can to give him the appropriate antibiotic therapy. He's also receiving intravenous fluids and oxygen along with narcotic painkillers.'

'What happens now? Will he be transferred out of here?'

'Yes, he'll be going to the intensive therapy unit just as soon as we have everything in place and we feel that he's ready to be moved.'

'Thank you,' Amelie said, and her gratitude was heartfelt. 'Thanks for everything that you've done for him. I know he's receiving the very best of care.' The surgeon was well respected among his colleagues, and she knew that Nathan was in excellent hands. Even so, the final outcome was a question of debate, and the possibility that he might not come through this was one she dared not contemplate.

'You must bear in mind that your brother is young, and that before this unfortunate event occurred he was relatively fit. That has to stand in his favour, as I'm sure you know, and we are doing everything we can to get him through this.'

'I know. I do appreciate all that you're doing for him.'

The surgeon gave her a kindly smile and made to leave. 'I'll keep you updated on your brother's condition, but if there's anything you want to ask in the meantime…if anything occurs to you…you can always come and find me at anytime.'

He left the room, and Gage said softly, 'Would you like to go and see your brother?'

She nodded. 'Yes, I need to see him. I feel so bad that this has come about, and that I didn't know anything of what he was going through.' She laid a hand on his arm. 'Oh, Gage, why didn't he tell me? He must have been in pain for some time before this happened.'

He drew her to him and held her close for a moment or two. 'I expect, like a lot of people, he thought it was something that would eventually pass. That's most likely why he stayed outside at the vet's place. He probably didn't like to lay his problems on anyone else and he thought he could work through it.'

'But I'm his sister,' she said in an anguished tone. 'He should have known that he could confide in me about anything.'

Gage lightly squeezed her shoulder, leading her out

of the waiting room. They went up to the recovery ward, and Amelie gazed at her brother as he lay in the hospital bed, the breath catching in her throat. He looked so ill, so vulnerable.

He wasn't responsive, even when she spoke quietly to him, and she realised that he didn't even know that she was there. He was still sedated, and she guessed that sleep was probably the best thing for him. At least that way he wasn't in too much pain.

'Shall I take you home?' Gage asked after a while. 'There's nothing more that you can do for him right now, is there?'

'But I'm so worried about him.' She looked at him, her mind in a whirl. 'I want to stay with him and be there at his bedside when he wakes up.' Amelie curled her fingers into small fists of frustration.

'I don't think he'll be making much sense for a while yet. He's still recovering from the anaesthetic, and it will be some time before he's fully alert. You would do better to go home and put Connor to bed and then try to get some sleep yourself. It's quite late. If we use my car, I could pick you up in the morning. I don't think you're in any state to drive.'

'I suppose you're right. Connor must be wondering what's happened to us, if he hasn't already fallen asleep.' She looked at her brother once more. 'I'll just leave Nathan a note in case he comes around and wants to know what's going on. I don't want him to think that I just abandoned him.'

Gage made a wry smile. 'I doubt that he would ever think that.'

They left the hospital a few minutes later, and Gage

drove her to Emma's father's house. He parked the car at the kerb outside the cottage, and went with her to collect Connor.

'He's asleep,' the grandad said, opening the door and ushering them both into the hallway. 'I left him on the settee watching a video while I cleared away the supper things, and he couldn't keep his eyes open any longer. He's been fine.'

He showed them through to the living room. 'How is Nathan doing?'

'Not too well at the moment, but they've operated on him and now he's in Intensive Care. They're going to let me know if there's any change at all.'

'I'm sorry. It must be a worrying time for you.'

She nodded. Emma's father had never had much time for Nathan, but at least he was sensitive enough to appreciate her feelings.

She looked at Connor. He was curled up on the settee, covered by a light blanket, and he had his thumb in his mouth just as he had when he'd been a baby settling down to sleep. Amelie's heart swelled with affection as she looked at him. However was she going to tell him that his father was dangerously ill?

'I'll carry him out to the car for you,' Gage said quietly. 'I'll do my best not to wake him. He looks as though he's sound asleep, so you may be able to get him to bed without too much trouble.'

'That would be good,' Amelie murmured. As he reached down to gently lift the child, she turned to his grandad. 'I don't know what I would have done without you. Thanks for looking after him.'

'You're welcome. I was glad to do it.' He patted her

arm awkwardly. 'I know this must have been a bad time for you. You know you can call on me any time you need me to help out.'

'I know. Thanks.' She realised that things must have been difficult for him, with his wife away, ill, and all the worry that entailed. Emma had told her that her mother was annoyed with him because of his continuing antagonism to the father of his grandchild, but still he had helped out.

Impulsively, she gave him a quick hug, and then looked to where Gage was waiting at the door. She straightened and went after him, following him outside. They drove towards her cottage.

'I've kept you away from your own home for an awfully long time,' she said, glancing at him as they turned into the back lane by the farm. 'I didn't mean to do that. I was just so wrapped up in what was happening that I didn't think.'

'Don't worry about it. After all, I offered to stay. It's been a difficult time for you. No one wants to see their loved ones hurt, and it helps to have someone by your side when you're going through something like this.'

'Thanks for being there for me. I don't think I could have managed without you.' It was true enough. His strength had kept her going through these last few dark hours. Without him she would have floundered for sure.

When he had parked the car outside her house, he lifted Connor from the back seat and carried the sleeping child into the cottage.

'Do you want me to take him upstairs for you? It might be less disturbing for him that way.'

'Thanks.' She showed him up to the smaller of the

two bedrooms. 'This is his room,' she told him. 'I'll pull the bedcovers back and if you lay him down I'll try to get him ready for bed without waking him.'

He did as she asked, lowering the boy gently onto the bed. Connor stirred and mumbled something incoherent and then drifted back to sleep.

'He's well away,' Gage murmured, his mouth tilting at the corners. 'I'll leave you to get him ready.' He walked to the door and then paused momentarily. 'You must be hungry,' he said. 'Neither of us has eaten anything since lunchtime. There's a Chinese take-away not too far away from here and I could go and fetch us something. Do you like Chinese food?'

'I love it, but I'm not actually very hungry at the moment.' She looked up, gently easing Connor's shoes from his feet.

'You ought to try to eat something. It will help to keep up your strength.'

'Maybe.' Her stomach felt as though it was wound up tight, and she wasn't sure that she could eat anything right now, but Gage had been good to her and perhaps she shouldn't put him off. 'Are you sure you don't mind going? I feel as though I've put upon you too much already.'

'I'm sure. I'll bring a selection.'

By the time she came downstairs some twenty or so minutes later, he was back with the meal. The smell was appetising and, despite her anxiety about her brother, she realised that she was tempted to try some of the food.

'We usually eat in the kitchen,' she murmured as she set out plates on the table. Now that he was here in her home, she was beginning to wonder what he made of it. 'It's often warmer in here, and anyway the living room is too small for me to be able to make room for a dining corner.'

She doubted that her tiny kitchen would come up to his standards, but it was the best that she could afford just now on her salary as a junior doctor. She still had loans to pay back to cover the expenses of her medical training.

Gage had pointed out his house to her when they had been on their way to the vet's surgery, and she had been impressed by its sheer size and the splendour of its land-scaped grounds. She had only seen it in passing, but there was no doubting that he lived in idyllic surroundings, and she guessed that the house was more of the same.

'I like it in here,' he said, looking around and admiring the scalloped blinds at the windows and the pine cupboards with their neat worktops. 'It has a homely feel to it.'

'Thanks.' The walls were a bright sunshine yellow, pleasing on the eye. She had arranged crockery on the Welsh dresser, and there were splashes of colour in the ceramics placed here and there about the room to make the place look cheerful.

He placed the foil containers in the centre of the table and started to remove the lids. 'Do your windows overlook the garden? It's too dark to be able to tell just now.'

'They do. It isn't a very big garden, and it's a bit scruffy right now, because I haven't had time to tend to it. A lot of the shrubs are overgrown, but it's well stocked, and I might be able to make something of it, given time.' She brought cutlery from a drawer, and set out knives and forks.

'You said that your house looks out over the bay,' she

murmured. 'You must have a fantastic view from where you're situated.'

'I do.' He produced a bottle of wine from one of the carrier bags and asked, 'Do you have any glasses, and a corkscrew? I shall have to limit what I drink because I'm driving, but there's nothing to stop you from enjoying it.'

She searched in the cupboard and brought out two crystal goblets. Her fingers traced the stems lightly, and then she quickly placed the glasses on the table. 'They were a house-warming present from my brother,' she explained. 'I've only used them once, to drink a toast with him when I moved in here.' There was a catch in her voice. 'I didn't imagine that our circumstances would change so quickly.'

'I know. You have to hold on to the fact that he's young and strong and that he can overcome this.'

She tried to do that. They sat down and helped themselves to the food, and she ate slowly, savouring it, while all the time her mind kept winging back to Nathan. 'Tell me about your house,' she said, seeking distraction, anything to stop her thoughts from straying.

'My brother and I inherited it from our grandparents,' he answered. 'I bought out my brother's half of the property because I really wanted to live there, and he wasn't so bothered about that. He has a place of his own in the city, nearer to where he works.'

'How did your parents feel about it? Were they glad to keep it in the family? They are still around, I take it?'

He laughed. 'Very much so. It used to be my mother's family home, and she was pleased that I kept it. My parents have a big house further along the coast, and I get to see them on a regular basis. Either I go to see them, or they come over to my place. I share my grandmother's love of the sea and I was always happy as a child, going to visit my grandparents. They would take me down to the beach to search for shells or to dabble in the rock pools. Sometimes we would go to the harbour and watch the fishermen working with the nets. It was a carefree time.'

'I used to feel much the same way about living near the coast.' Her eyes clouded. 'I'm not sure that I have the same view of it now. Since I nearly drowned I've been nervous about going to the beach. It's unfortunate, because Connor keeps asking me to take him there.'

He scanned her features. 'I suppose it was almost inevitable that you would feel that way.'

She nodded. 'Tell me some more about the house. I thought it was beautiful, even from a distance. It was long and white and all different levels, with angled roofs and square-paned windows and so many flowers giving it colour. It sort of draws the eye.'

Gage twisted noodles around his fork, accepting her change of subject easily enough. 'My grandmother chose the house specially. She said that she fell in love with it as soon as she saw it, and once she set foot inside she knew that it had to be hers. My grandfather obliged her by buying it.'

He smiled and stopped to take a sip of his wine. 'They were a lovely couple. As to the house itself, I have a breakfast room that overlooks the little fishing harbour, and I often sit by the window and watch the boats coming in, laden with the morning's catch.'

'It sounds wonderful.'

'It is. I'm very fortunate.'

She speared a fork full of spicy chicken and asked, 'What do your parents do? Do they both work?'

He nodded. 'My father is a doctor, a GP, and my mother is a midwife. You could say that I was born into medicine. It's all I've known, and it's all I ever wanted to do.'

'And your brother?'

'He works in investment banking. Quite different from the rest of us, but he has a quick mind and he's very good in the world of finance. He gives out sound advice.'

'Perhaps I should have a talk with him,' she said with a wry twist to her mouth. 'My finances could do with some adjustment.'

He gave her an answering smile. 'I'm sure we could arrange something.' He sent her a quick glance. 'Do you want to tell me some more about your family? You said that your father had been in touch recently. Have you decided what you're going to do about that?'

Amelie shook her head. 'Nathan didn't reply to the letter, as far as I know. He was still making up his mind what he ought to do about it.'

'Don't you think you should get in touch with your father now that Nathan's ill? I know how you feel about him, but doesn't he have a right to know what's happening to his son?'

A faint note of irony entered her voice. 'I don't recall my dad keeping in touch with us to find out whether we were well or ill while we were growing up. I don't feel that we owe him any loyalty.'

He looked at her doubtfully. 'Circumstances change. You might find that you come to regret it if you don't make an effort to contact him.'

She threw him a sharp look. 'If anything happens to Nathan, you mean?'

'No, I didn't mean that. I mean that family relationships are important. You might be trying to deny what you really feel deep down. People make mistakes, they argue and fall out, but it can be good try to smooth things over. I've had some dealings with your father over the last few months and, no matter what he's done in the past, he comes across as a decent man now. You might find that he wants to make amends for how he was then.'

Amelie frowned. 'You're asking me to forgive him, but I can't do that. He had a family, and he chose to leave us behind and forget about us when it suited him. He was more interested in building up his business, and he thought that he could leave my mother and play the field with other women as he pleased. He was selfish. All he wanted was to enjoy the best of both worlds.'

'I understand that, but he might be regretting his behaviour by now. After all, he made the effort to get in touch. People do sometimes change and have different priorities as they grow older.'

She looked at him directly. 'You don't know what you're asking of me. I'm not ready to forgive and forget.'

'Your brother might feel differently. Illness is a great leveller.'

'I don't think so,' she said tersely. How could he even suggest that she make up with her father? When it came down to it, Gage wasn't any different from all the other men, was he? Didn't they always side with each other? Why should they let a little emotional difficulty get in the way of things? 'As far as Nathan's concerned, I think it's more important that I contact his girlfriend and let her know what's happened.' She grimaced. 'Emma's gone away for a few days, but she might want to come home early if she knows that Nathan is unwell. I suppose it depends whether her mother's health is any better and whether she feels able to leave her.'

She pushed her plate away and surveyed the remains of the meal. They had made inroads into every item, and it had satisfied her hunger, but now she wanted it cleared away out of sight. She wished she could sweep away the debris from her mind just as easily.

Perhaps he read her thoughts. 'I should go,' he said, getting to his feet. 'I'll help you tidy up, and then I'll leave you in peace. You look all in. It's been a long day.'

She nodded. 'You're right. I shouldn't have kept you all this while. You're on early shift tomorrow, aren't you?'

'That's true, but, then, so are you, unless you're taking time out because of what's happened to your brother?' His tone was flat, and she guessed that he was disturbed by her sudden change of mood.

'No, I'm coming in to work. I'll be closer to him there.'

'You should try to get some rest, then. You probably have a difficult day ahead of you. I'll come and pick you up first thing.'

He didn't say very much more, keeping his comments brief and to the point. When he left the house just a short time later, she had the impression that he was mulling over what she had said.

She was already regretting her outburst. All had been going well until he had mentioned her father, and she guessed that was the flashpoint that had started the slow burn of resentment in her. Guilt washed over her. It had been unfair to vent her irritability on him. He didn't deserve to be treated that way.

Gage had been good to her, supporting her, being there for her when she had been at her lowest ebb, and how had she thanked him? She had turned him away, and berated him for his attempts at peacemaking.

Unhappy and disgruntled, she went upstairs. Connor was sleeping peacefully, and she kissed his forehead and lightly stroked his hair before going into her own room to prepare for bed. She spent a restless night, tossing and turning, reliving the nightmare of her brother's collapse.

In the morning, she woke much later than she had intended, and was horrified to discover that she had slept through the alarm. After that it was a rush to get herself and Connor ready for the day ahead.

'When's my daddy coming home?' Connor asked. 'Grandad said his tummy was poorly. Is it still hurting him?'

'I'm afraid so,' she told him, anxiety flooding through her as she tried to explain. 'He has to stay in bed for a while in the hospital, until the doctors can make him better again. I don't think he'll be coming home for a few days yet, but as soon as he's feeling a little bit better, I'll take you to see him, I promise.'

She had phoned the hospital first thing, and so far Nathan's condition had not changed. She didn't know whether that was a good or a bad thing. At any rate, the nursing team was still very worried about him.

Connor was not appeased. 'I want to see my mummy,' he said. 'When is she coming home?'

'In a few days' time, all being well,' Amelie answered. 'You spoke to her on the phone yesterday, didn't you? Your teacher told me that she called you at lunch-time. Didn't she tell you that she would be coming home soon?'

'She did. She said Grandma was getting better. Grandma was tired, and she needed a few days in bed, Mummy said. She said Grandad was getting on her nerves and Grandma needed...' He screwed up his nose as he tried to think what it was that his mother had said. 'A bit of space.' He looked up at Amelie. 'Did she mean that Grandma needed to stay away from Grandad for a while?'

'I think that's probably about it,' Amelie agreed. 'Sometimes grown-ups can be a bit silly.'

He nodded wisely. 'Especially Grandad. He tells my mummy, "You should stay away from that man...he's nothing but trouble. It's time you learned some sense, my girl."' He made a face. 'He means Daddy, but my daddy's not trouble, is he? And my mummy's got lots of sense. She knows her twelve times table, and she knows all about how to make paper kites.' His eyes grew large with the enormity of that.

'Well, that's what's important, isn't it?' Amelie murmured. 'Where would we be without times tables and kites?'

Gage arrived a few minutes later, just as they were finishing breakfast. Amelie went to let him in.

'Come into the kitchen,' she murmured. 'We're just about ready to go.' To Connor, she said, 'Finish up your toast, Connor. Gage is waiting to take me in to work.'

Connor looked up at Gage, studying him closely for a moment or two. 'Is you a doctor?' he asked.

'Yes, I am,' Gage answered.

'Do you wear a listening thing round your neck?'

'A stethoscope? Yes, I do.'

Connor seemed satisfied with that for the moment. He finished eating his toast and then carefully brushed the crumbs away. 'Look,' he said, pulling at his T-shirt and showing it to Amelie. 'No jam today.'

'Well, that is good news,' she said, giving him a smile.

The child grinned and while she went to get his coat, he said to Gage, 'She said her boss would be cross if she was late for work, but I got jam on my T-shirt and she had to find another one, and she said, "I don't know where all this washing comes from. I think these T-shirts breed in the wash bin."' He put his head to one side and pursed his lips. 'What does "breed" mean?'

Gage stifled a laugh. 'It means they're getting together and making more than one, and then she has a lot more washing to do.'

'Oh.' Connor's brows drew together, but he seemed satisfied with that answer for the time being.

'We should go,' Amelie said, bringing Connor's coat, and they went outside to where Gage's car was parked.

Connor's eyes widened. 'Is this yours?' he asked in an awe-struck tone, looking up at Gage.

'Yes, it is.'

His face broke into a wide smile. 'It's wicked. I love it.' His eyes sparkled as he surveyed the beautiful silver saloon.

'In you get,' Gage said, 'and I'll drive you to school.'

Connor looked at Amelie for confirmation of that, and when she nodded, he whooped with joy. He didn't need a second bidding but scrambled inside and bounced into the back seat. 'Whey-hey, this is well good.'

Amelie winced for the upholstery under the onslaught of grubby shoes, but Gage didn't seem to mind. 'Buckle up,' he said. He seemed totally relaxed, and she settled in the passenger seat beside him, sending him a thoughtful glance. She had never known a man like Gage before. He took everything in his stride and nothing seemed to throw him off balance. He was good to be around.

Some half an hour later, after they had dropped Connor off at school, she stopped by to look in on Nathan. He looked dreadful, pale and debilitated. He managed to say a few words to her, but he wasn't really in any condition to have visitors and she was desperately afraid that the antibiotics weren't working. She was devastated to see him looking so ill. How was she going to be able to explain things to Connor?

The nurse took her to one side. 'We're keeping him on oxygen therapy,' she told her, 'and we're giving him something to slow his heart rate. He's really very poorly.'

'I know. Thank you for taking care of him so well. I'll come back and see him at lunchtime, if I may?'

'Of course.'

Feeling upset and frazzled before she had even made a start, Amelie hurried back down to A and E. Gage was already at work, attending to a man who had suffered a stroke.

'Is there no change in your brother's condition?' he asked, moving away from the patient's bedside and coming towards her.

'Not so far.' She started towards the desk, and he went with her.

'I'm sorry. I'm sure you were hoping that the news would be better.' He made a face. 'You should go and visit him whenever you feel the need, you know. We'll sort something out down here.'

'Thanks. I'll go and see him in my break times, otherwise I'll wait for the nurse to call me if there's any change.'

He studied her. 'Have you been in touch with his girlfriend?'

'Not yet. I've tried ringing her, but so far I haven't been able to get through.'

It was something she would have to deal with, along with making arrangements for Connor to be collected from school. Perhaps she would do better to find out if the children's day care unit at the hospital would find him a place for a few days if there was going to be any delay until Emma returned.

The specialist registrar came to find Gage just then. 'Did you manage to find cover for when you and I go off on the new surgical techniques course? It's going to go on for a couple of days and lately we don't seem to be able to get replacements to fill in on these occasions, do we?'

'I suppose we'll just have to cross that bridge when we come to it,' Gage said. 'I'll do what I can to make adequate arrangements. You can't simply drop out, because it's part of your specialist training and you need to get the session in before the end of the month.'

Amelie frowned. She remembered that there had been talk of the course a couple of weeks ago. It was a residential one, being held at a conference hotel some fifty miles away. She hadn't realised that Gage and Gina were going to be attending it together.

Gage looked at Gina once more. 'Have you had time to look over the literature they sent us with the tickets?' he asked.

Gina pulled a face. 'I have, but I can't say that I made much sense of it. Some of it seemed to be in very technical language. I was going to ask you what you thought about it... I'd feel happier if you could go over the papers with me some time.'

He nodded. 'It could have been simplified. We could meet up after work and go through them, if you like.'

'That would be great, thanks.' Gina's mouth widened, a smile lighting her eyes. 'Do you want to come over to my place?'

'OK.'

Amelie pulled out a case file from the stack. Somehow, her day had just taken a turn for the worse, but for the life of her she couldn't fathom the reason for the sudden drop in her spirits. Why should it bother her that Gage and the registrar were meeting up after work?

It wasn't as though she had any intention of letting herself fall for him, was it...even if he had kissed her that one time and turned her blood to flame? She knew better than to give her heart away to any man, didn't she?

Gage's voice broke into her thoughts. 'You won't get very far with that case,' he said briskly, glancing at the file she was holding.

Amelie stared at him. 'Why do you say that? I don't know what you mean.' Had he picked up on her distraction? Wasn't there anything he missed?

'You're holding it upside down,' he pointed out. 'It usually helps if you have things the right way up.'

She stared at the offending folder and her mouth dropped open when she saw that he was right. Quickly, she turned the chart around, sending him a stiff glance. 'I was thinking about something else,' she said.

'Hmm.' He gave her a quizzical look and went off to find his next patient.

CHAPTER SEVEN

'MRS FRANKLIN'S husband is in the waiting room with their two young children,' Chloe said in an undertone, coming into the treatment cubicle and taking Amelie to one side. 'Is there any news?'

Amelie shook her head. 'Not so far, but I'll go and have a word with him in a little while. She's very poorly, and I'm still waiting on results. I've requested blood cultures, along with a full blood count, urea and electrolytes.' She glanced at Chloe. 'Are you taking over her care while the duty nurse is at lunch?'

'Yes. In fact, I'm here for the rest of the afternoon.'

'Good. Keep a check on her urine output for me, will you, and let me know if the ECG trace changes?'

'I will.' Chloe checked the patient's chart. 'What about antibiotics? Are you prescribing any?'

'Until the culture results come back, I've no way of knowing which ones to give her, but we'll start her with a broad-spectrum antibiotic to be on the safe side.' She pressed her lips together. 'She's very weak.'

'Is it food poisoning?' Chloe asked.

'I believe so. We'll probably need to notify environmental health just as soon as we know exactly what's causing the trouble. She's going downhill very fast, but at least the intravenous fluids will do something to help prevent her from going into shock. I think she should have an anti-emetic, too. The vomiting isn't doing her any good. I'm worried about her.'

It was upsetting, watching this woman suffering from such a toxic overload. It reminded Amelie of how her brother was suffering, and it added to her feeling of helplessness. Nathan was still desperately ill and there was nothing she could do to influence his recovery.

'Her children are so young,' Chloe said. 'The father's doing his best to keep their spirits up, but you can tell that he's scared to death.'

'I can imagine how he must be feeling.' Amelie felt the weight of responsibility on her. She would do everything she could to ensure that those children would not lose their mother. 'It's frightening to know how quickly something like this can pull a person down, but I think she was frail before this. She was just getting over a virus of some sort and it left her weak. Her condition is really beginning to make me concerned.'

'Do you want me to try and get hold of Gage?'

'No. He's working with a road accident victim and I don't want to disturb him over this unless I really have to.'

'Oh, I see. I wasn't sure whether they had finished dealing with all the casualties. They've been working on them all morning and Gina said she hadn't even had time to stop for a break since she came in first thing.'

'It has been hectic.' Amelie pulled her mind swiftly back to her patient. 'I do need to involve a specialist, though,' she told Chloe. 'It looks as though Mrs Franklin is going into renal failure, and I'm battling against time.

I'm thinking we should call in Dr Trent from the renal unit. It may be that if her serum potassium level continues to rise, we'll have to put her on dialysis until her condition improves.'

'All right.' Chloe sent her a quick look. 'How are you bearing up?'

'I'm fine.'

James came and found her later on in the afternoon as she was treating an asthma patient. 'Gage wants you to come and help out with a trauma patient in the next bay,' he said. 'You're due to go off duty soon, though, aren't you?'

'Yes, but it's OK. I'll come straight away.' To the girl she was treating, she said, 'Just keep the oxygen mask in place. We're giving you nebulised salbutamol, and it will help you to breathe more easily.' She moved away from the patient's bedside and a nurse came to take her place.

She walked with James along the corridor towards the next bay, and said, 'I thought Gage was working with Gina today?'

'He was, but she's gone to follow up on some results.'

She had told herself that Gage's private life was none of her business, but her curiosity had been getting the better of her ever since she had heard that he was meeting up with Gina after work the other day. Now she said, 'They've been working together a lot of late, haven't they? Is that because she has to take specialist exams soon?'

James nodded. 'I think so. That's one reason why he's supervising her so carefully, but they also have a history, from what I've heard. Apparently they were at medical school together and they were very close. I don't think much has changed there.'

'No, that's probably true.' It wasn't what she wanted to hear, and she was filled with a sense of despondency, of an ache starting up in the pit of her stomach. She had been right to be wary of getting too close to him, hadn't she?

They reached the cubicle where Gage was attending to the patient.

'Good. There you are,' he said, flicking a glance over them as they walked in. He indicated the patient, who was propped up on the bed. 'This is Martin Graham. He's had an unfortunate accident, and I have to reduce a Colles' fracture. It means that I need to do a Bier's block to anaesthetise his hand.'

He added in a low voice, 'We need two doctors to be present in case of side effects from the anaesthetic.'

Amelie nodded. 'OK.'

'James, I want you to observe, and see to it that Martin's other injuries don't cause too many problems. He has rib fractures as well as the fracture of the wrist.'

James looked at the patient. 'That sounds as though you were very unlucky.'

Mr Graham winced. 'Yes, I think I was, though I suppose it could have been much worse. I slid off a roof where I was working and broke my fall on a closed local authority refuse bin. Then I bounced off that and landed on my hand.'

'Ouch!' Amelie sympathised.

'He might need an intercostal nerve block for the rib injuries,' Gage murmured, 'but we can't do that at the same time.'

A moment later, he was ready to start the procedure. 'I'm going to insert a small IV cannula in the dorsum of the hand,' Gage said as he prepared the anaesthetic.

'We'll need to place another one in the opposite arm.'
Lowering his voice, he added for James's benefit,
'That's in case of an emergency. If there's a severe toxic
reaction to the anaesthetic, we need to be able to resuscitate the patient.'

He checked the radial pulse and placed the tourniquet
high on the arm. 'All right, we're going to elevate the
arm for a few minutes.' To Amelie, he said, 'I'll inflate
the tourniquet. Will you record the time, and observe the
pressure?'

She nodded. Slowly, Gage injected the anaesthetic
into the limb, and tested that it was doing its job. Once
he was satisfied, he asked James to help while he ma-
nipulated the fracture.

'How are you doing?' he asked the patient, observ-
ing him closely.

'I'm OK.' The man looked a little apprehensive, but
so far there was no sign of any untoward effects.

'That's good.' Gage removed the cannula and
glanced at James. 'We'll apply a backslab to keep the
hand in the correct position.'

'Shall I start to release the tourniquet?' Amelie asked
after a few minutes.

Gage nodded. 'Be careful how you go. Do it slowly.'
He looked at Martin once more. 'Is the sensation return-
ing to your arm?'

'Yes, it feels warm.'

'Good. We'll move you on to the recovery ward in a
while, and a nurse will keep an eye on you over the next
couple of hours. Once we're satisfied that all's well and
the circulation is as it should be, we'll decide what to
do about the rib fractures. It may be that we can do

something for you to provide more local relief for the pain, but it will mean that you have to be admitted to hospital so that we can keep a close check on you.'

'I'm OK with that. I don't think I'll be going back up on the roof any time soon.'

Gage laughed. 'I think I'd agree with you there, but it was a bit of a drastic way to get time off work, don't you think? I should try for a simple stomach bug next time, if I were you.'

The patient managed a wry smile, and when the nurse came to move him to Recovery, James went with them.

'Are you about ready to go off home now?' Gage asked, as he and Amelie cleared away.

She nodded. 'I'm going to collect Connor from nursery school, and I said I would take him with me to see Nathan after I finish work. I don't know quite how he's going to react to seeing him so ill. As it is, he's been a bit fractious lately, but I suppose it's to be expected. His routine has been upset, with one thing and another. I'm still waiting for a place in day care for him.'

'Could you try distracting him with something afterwards, to take his mind off things?' His gaze settled on her. 'Didn't you say that he's been asking you to take him down to the beach? It's a beautiful day today, and the sun's still shining, so it would be a good time to do that.'

'I'm not sure.' She sent him a fleeting, doubtful glance. 'I've been thinking about taking him, but I haven't quite been able to get up the nerve to do it. I managed to drive by the cove a couple of times, and I stepped out of the car to go and walk down there, but every time I get close I want to turn and run.'

He smiled and touched her arm lightly in a consoling gesture. 'At least you tried.' He watched the expressions flit across her face. 'Perhaps you should start by going to a different part of the beach. The bay near where I live is wide and less threatening perhaps. I've nearly finished here, and I could go with you, if you like. If you find it too difficult, we could come away.'

'But then Connor would miss out.'

'Not necessarily. If you feel you don't want to stay there, you could relax for a while at my house and I'll take him to the beach. What do you say?'

'Would you do that?' She gave it some thought. 'I suppose I could try. I don't want to let Connor down.'

'Good girl. I'll come and find you later on, and we'll make a trip of it. I could scramble a picnic together for us. I think I have buckets and spades stashed away somewhere from when my brother's children came to visit.'

She smiled at him. 'You think of everything, don't you? I'm still struggling to get past the thought of going there at all.'

'You'll be fine. I'll take care of you both, so you don't need to worry.'

He made it sound so easy, but when she went off duty she still doubted whether she had made the right decision. She went and picked up Connor and took him to see his dad, preparing him for the visit as best she could.

Connor's expression was solemn as they came away a few minutes later. 'My daddy's very poorly, isn't he? He looks a funny colour and he didn't say very much. I want my mummy to come home.'

'I know you do, sweetheart,' Amelie said, giving him a cuddle. 'I'm sure she'll be back with you soon.'

Connor shook his head. 'She phoned me at school

today and I telled her I wanted her to come home and she said, yes, but Grandma had a poorly heart and she has to stay in bed and she can't leave her just yet.' His lower lip trembled. 'I want to see my grandma.'

'You will, soon.' Obviously the message Amelie had left for Emma had not been passed on. 'If your mummy isn't home by Friday, I'll take you up to Launceston to see her.'

He seemed to be content with that for the moment, and Amelie was relieved. As they walked out into the corridor, she saw that Gage was waiting for them.

'Hi, Connor,' he said. 'How are you doing?'

'A'right.' Connor pulled a toy soldier from his pocket and began to play with it.

Gage put an arm around Amelie and gave her shoulder a light squeeze. 'You look subdued,' he said in a quiet voice. 'How is your brother?'

'He's not doing too well.' She was glad about that steadying hand. It made her feel secure, protected, as though she wasn't alone in this. 'The doctor's still concerned about him, and he's decided to add another antibiotic to the mixture. He's being given an intravenous infusion so that the treatment will work faster. We can't do anything more but wait.'

'I'm sorry. I know it must be hard for you.'

'He's worrying about things…about Emma and the problems he was having at work.'

'About the animals escaping, you mean?'

'That's right. Ill as he is, it seems to be playing on his mind. He still can't accept that he was responsible, and he wants to know how it happened.' She made a face. 'The trouble is, there haven't been any similar incidents since he came into hospital. It makes things look bad for him.'

'I suppose it would.' He frowned. 'I suppose it's always possible that he made a mistake. His illness could have contributed to his being careless.'

She stiffened. 'I don't believe that.'

'No, but, then, again, you're his sister, and you're probably biased.' Gage was thoughtful for a moment. 'Couldn't they rig up some kind of video surveillance to find out what's been going on? That might help to clarify things a bit.'

'It would, wouldn't it? I'll mention it to Lewis.'

Gage's eyes took on a brooding expression that she didn't fully understand, but he said nothing more on the matter and turned his attention to Connor, who was fidgeting by her side. 'So, Connor,' he said, hunkering down to be on a level with the little boy, 'How do you feel about going down to the beach? I put some buckets and spades in my car. What do you think of that?'

'Today?' Connor's eyes lit up. 'Oh, yes. Can I paddle in the sea?' He looked up at Amelie. 'Can I?'

Amelie felt a chill sweep through her as memories of that last day on the beach came back to haunt her. 'I don't know about paddling. We'll see,' she said.

Gage straightened up and drew her close to him, and a tinge of warmth crept back where his hand rested lightly on her waist. 'Take it easy,' he murmured. 'There's no reason to panic.'

She looked at him warily. She wasn't so sure about that. He was being good to her, helping her out, and all the time she felt herself falling, little by little, under his spell. It shouldn't be happening at all, though, should it? She ought to guard against letting herself have any feelings for him. Deep down she knew that she could end up regretting it.

They headed down the corridor towards the lifts. 'We'll drop your car off at the cottage first, shall we?'

She nodded. 'I need to pick up a few things from there.' She still couldn't work out why Gage would want to put himself out this way. Then again, he had been good with Connor from the outset, and perhaps the two of them had built up a rapport.

At the cottage, she thought about hanging back and putting off the trip until another day, but that wasn't really an option, was it, with Connor jumping about with excitement?

Once she was sitting in Gage's car, though, she gradually absorbed the relaxing opulence of the interior and let the smooth hum of the engine lull her into acceptance. It occurred to her that this was the reason he had insisted on driving them himself. He didn't want her to have an excuse to back out.

Gage found a parking spot at the top of the cliff, and they stood for a moment and admired the view. In the distance, there was a small harbour to one side of the bay, where fishing boats bobbed gently on the water and nets and crab pots lined the quayside. Nearer to them was a landing stage where fishermen could haul the boats onto the shore. Amelie held Connor's hand, and pointed out the gulls that circled the bay.

'They go in search of fish at the harbour,' she told him. 'This must be their favourite place.'

Connor laughed. 'Mine's down there,' he said, pointing to the long stretch of golden sand below them.

The sea was a perfect blue, rolling in gently and lapping at the beach, leaving white breakers of foam to dissolve on the shore.

'Let's go, then, shall we?' Gage said. He had lifted the buckets and spades out of the boot, and he was holding a wicker basket in his other hand.

'What's in there?' Connor asked, as they found the path and started to make their way down the cliff.

'Some food.' Gage looked at him. 'Are you hungry?'

Connor nodded vigorously. 'I'm starving. Are there any biscuits? I like jammy ones.'

'Biscuits, sandwiches and some fresh chicken. There are some apples and oranges, too, and some juice.'

'Can we eat it now?'

Gage smiled. 'When we get down to the beach. Look, we need to go down the steps now. We'll find a place nearby where we can sit, and we can set the basket down on the wall.' Gage looked at Amelie. 'If we do that, you'll have an escape route if you should need it,' he murmured.

She pulled in a steadying breath and looked about her. He was right. This spot was just perfect, close to the exit from the beach, with a flat-topped stone wall at the edge to provide a table for their picnic.

A few people were enjoying the beach. The day was still warm, and one or two children had ventured into the water and were splashing about.

Gage set the wicker basket down on the wall and opened it up. 'What would you like?' he asked, glancing at Amelie. 'Yoghurt? You can have strawberry or cherry, or there's fresh fruit salad, and there are cheese or ham sandwiches. Help yourself.'

'How on earth did you manage to put all this together so quickly?' she asked in astonishment. 'You finished work after me, didn't you?'

He shrugged. 'Some of it was in my fridge at home, and the rest is courtesy of the supermarket. I didn't know whether you'd prefer wine or juice or milk, so I brought all three to be on the safe side.'

Amelie chuckled and bit into a sandwich. 'This is wonderful. It's the best picnic I have ever had.'

'I'm glad about that.' His eyes were dark as his gaze shifted over her. 'I thought you could do with a break.' He cut a slice of chocolate cake and handed it to her on a serviette. 'Eat up. You could do with putting some meat on your bones. You've lost weight.'

'I haven't.' She looked down at herself, checking the waistband of her jeans, which, to her surprise, was a little looser than usual. 'Have I?' She stared at him. 'How would you know that?'

'I treated you when you first came into the hospital, remember? We had to take your wet things off you, so it was really hard not to notice that you were actually quite perfect in every way. It would be such a shame to see you waste away.'

'O-oh…' Her mouth dropped open and she stared at him, her eyes widening. He had seen her without her clothes… 'Oh…'

He smiled crookedly. 'Don't let it bother you. I'm just saying that you should eat up and get yourself back to how you were.' His gaze wandered over her. 'You're beautiful, Amelie. Don't you know that?'

'Oh…' she said again. She closed her mouth and darted a quick look at Connor. He was oblivious to their conversation, thank heaven, stuffing his mouth full of bread and searching in the basket for any other goodies that might be to hand.

Then he turned and looked at her and said, 'Can I go and paddle in the sea now?'

She was almost thankful for the distraction, but she looked into the distance where the waves were slowly breaking onto the shore and a feeling of panic welled up in her. 'I...I don't think that's a good idea,' she managed, 'and we don't have a towel.' It wasn't exactly an oversight on her part. Back at the house, when she'd had the chance to collect whatever she might need, she had shied away at the last moment from the thought of going anywhere near the water's edge.

'I could take him,' Gage said. 'We've plenty of paper towels in the basket to dry him off, and there's a blanket in the car if we need it. I could always put that round him later.' His gaze held hers, warm and steady.

'All right.' She swallowed. It was disconcerting, having him look at her in that direct, all-seeing way, but perhaps she was being over-sensitive after the conversation they had just shared. Did he really like the way she looked?

He stood up. 'Do you want to come with us?' He held out a hand to her and she stared at it, but held back. She started to shake her head.

'Please,' Connor begged. 'I want you to come with us...please?' He wanted to share every part of this time on the beach, but still she hesitated.

'I don't know.'

Gage caught hold of her hand and carefully pulled her to her feet. 'You'll be all right,' he said. 'I won't let you go.' He watched her reaction and added softly, 'You don't want Connor to pick up on your fear, do you?'

She pulled in another long breath. 'I don't think I want to be that close to the water.'

'I know you don't, but it'll be fine, you'll see.'

She didn't believe it, but all the same she let him lead her across the sand to the water's edge. 'Shoes and socks off. Grab a bucket, Connor,' Gage said. 'We'll build a castle with a moat and we'll need water to go around it.'

Connor didn't need to be told twice. He hopped and skipped all the way to the water and when they reached the water's edge he laughed as the waves tumbled over his bare feet.

Amelie watched him as he curled his toes into the wet sand. He waded out deeper into the sea, until it was up to his knees, and she was beginning to be afraid for him, knowing that she needed to go after him in case of danger, but somehow she was frozen to the spot and couldn't move.

Her heart was thumping, partly from anxiety and the rest from the knowledge that Gage was holding her hand firmly in his. He hadn't let go, as he had promised, but she knew that she couldn't allow him to leave Connor to wander unchecked. She had to let him release her, but for the moment she just couldn't find the courage to do it.

Then Connor tumbled, and her heart stopped, and all at once she was running towards him, scooping him up out of the water before he could utter his first stunned gasp.

'Are you all right?' she asked him, and the child nodded, getting his breath back, and it was clear that he was shocked and didn't know whether to laugh or cry. In the end, safe in her arms, he laughed up at her.

'I'm wet,' he said. 'Look at me, I'm wet all over.'

'So you are, but it doesn't matter.'

He started to jump up and down, exuberant with the heady delight of this new pastime.

Amelie was getting splashed as well, and she suddenly realised that she was standing in the sea, and that no one was holding on to her. Her jeans were soaked through to the knee, and she could feel the weight of the fabric flapping against her legs. She half turned, but Gage was by her side, and he was watching her cautiously, a question in his gaze.

'Are you all right?'

She nodded, too breathless from the shock of what had just happened for her to be able to speak for the moment.

He said softly, 'You know, when you rescued that man with the broken leg, you had no qualms about what you were doing. You were in the sea, and you stayed with him the whole time and didn't think about leaving him and trying to save yourself. And now the sea is peaceful and calm, so you have to ask yourself, What is there to be afraid of?'

'I think you've just said it all, haven't you?' she answered quietly. 'The point is, when the man was hurt, I simply didn't think beyond the moment. I just did what had to be done, and it's only now, when I have time to look back and reflect on it, that I realise how terrible it actually was.'

'How are you feeling now?'

'I feel…better… I think that I'm not so scared all at once.' She looked at Connor, splashing about in the water, running in and out of the sea and squealing with delight, and she gave a faint smile. 'I'm not convinced that I'll feel entirely comfortable being by the sea, but I'll probably be all right from now on.'

He hugged her close. 'I'm glad. I'm really pleased for you.' He looked ahead, to follow Connor's antics in the water and added, 'I think I'd better capture that young man and get him building sandcastles, or we'll never get him out of there and dry once more. Perhaps I'd better shoot back to the car and bring the blanket down here. Shall we all go together?'

She nodded. 'I'll take those wet things off him and he can wear my jacket. I left it in the back of your car.'

Once they had done that, they spent another hour on the beach, building an elaborate castle with a moat and a wall of shells and pebbles to keep out the enemy. Connor was happy, but he was starting to become tired, and eventually they made their way back to Gage's house.

'I'll see if I can find some clothes for him,' Gage said, when he had shown them into the living room. 'My nephew's about his size, and I keep some spare clothes on hand in case the children come to stay overnight. They like to sleep over sometimes at the weekend when their parents come down to the beach.' He waved a hand towards the sofa. 'Make yourself comfortable. Connor might like to rummage through the children's toy box in the corner.'

Connor went to examine the damask-covered box, while Amelie looked about her. The living room was long and wide, with almost ceiling-to-floor windows on two sides, and patio doors leading out to a terrace. There was an open fireplace with a slate hearth, and the floor was oak, but covered with luxurious Chinese rugs. The furniture was ultra-comfortable, inviting her to sit on the well-padded, beautifully upholstered settee, and there were plants dotted about the room, adding splashes of green, with warm tones of ruby, orange and yellow in the flower arrangements.

Gage came back after a while with a selection of T-shirts, trousers, socks and underwear, and Amelie hurried to get Connor dressed.

'I'll make us some coffee,' Gage murmured, and disappeared into the kitchen. When he came back a few minutes later, he placed a tray on the top of a writing desk to one side of the room and offered her a cup. 'Drink up, and I'll show you around, if you like,' he said.

'I would, thank you. What I've seen so far is lovely.'

Connor stayed in the living room, playing with cars on a specially printed mat, and Gage led Amelie on a tour of the house. She was overwhelmed by it all. The rooms were large and tastefully decorated, with deep-pile carpets in the bedrooms and expertly designed curtains framing the windows. The kitchen was a dream come true of cream units and wall-mounted shelving, with a table and chairs in one corner by the window and a tiled floor.

'This is all so beautiful,' Amelie breathed, leaning back against the corner unit. 'I'm not surprised that you wanted to keep it.'

'I'm glad you like it,' he said with a twist to his mouth, coming over to her, 'and it's great to see you looking a bit more relaxed.' He looked down into her eyes and drew her to him. 'Are you feeling better about our trip out? I know you had your doubts about it.'

'I'm glad that I let you persuade me in the end,' she murmured, gazing up at him. It felt good to have him hold her this way. It seemed right, somehow, and she was conscious of the warmth of his long body close to hers, of the way his eyes were smiling down at her.

'The fresh air has done you a world of good. There's colour in your cheeks and I'm pleased about that.' He ran a finger lightly down her cheek and then leaned towards her, and she tentatively let her hand glide over his rib cage. He was so strong and masculine, and she thrilled to feel the heavy thud of his heart beneath her fingers. She wanted him to hold her tight, to bring her nearer, much nearer to him, but it seemed as though he was holding himself back.

She sent him a fleeting, wondering glance, and then he made a soft groan in the back of his throat and tugged her close, claiming her lips in a fervent, heartfelt kiss. A tremor of heat ran through her, surging through her veins and bringing her pulses to clamouring life.

Her lips softened and parted and perhaps one kiss just wasn't enough, because her mind was willing her body closer to his until she felt the pressure of his thigh against hers. His smouldering gaze enveloped her and he kissed her again, and this time he didn't release her. His lips moved persuasively on hers, passionately, lighting a fuse within her. Sweet sensation sizzled through her, sparking from her lips to the tips of her toes, and she melted against him, loving the way his body crushed hers, the way her breasts softened against the hard expanse of his chest.

His hands stroked her, moving over her spine, her hips, smoothing over every curve and hollow, inciting her to return his kisses with ever-growing excitement. She wanted this so much; she was in desperate need of these hands tracing a delicious path over her body, cupping the swell of her hips and urging her to him.

'You taste of chocolate and juice and all things sweet and tempting,' he murmured against her cheek. 'I don't know how I've managed to resist you for so long.' He placed a row of kisses along the curve of her throat. 'What am I going to do about you?'

She tried to think about that, but her mind was whirling and she couldn't quite make the transition from the heady clouds of desire to the level plains of coherent thought. Why did he have to do anything at all...except kiss her and make her forget about everything that was troublesome in her life? Here in his arms she was safe, sheltered from any kind of hurt.

She frowned. Wasn't that it...the hurting? Wasn't there some reason why she needed to be cautious about getting up close and personal with him?

Whatever it was, it had escaped her for now, and she contented herself with easing back from him a little and gazing distractedly into his eyes. 'I can't think straight,' she said. 'I'm confused, and I think perhaps I should take a moment to get myself back together.'

His hand lightly cupped her face, his thumb tracing a path along the line of her jaw. 'That's a shame. I think I like you this way, all bemused and dreamy. There's plenty of time for order and precision at work.'

Work...was that it? Was that was what was bothering her? The answer hit her like a thunderbolt. Wasn't there a problem there, with a woman who had a history with him? How up to date was that history, and why was he playing fast and loose with her, if that was the case? Wasn't he acting in exactly the same way that her father behaved, flitting from one woman to another?

'I finished playing with the cars,' a small voice said. There was a patter of feet, and Connor asked plaintively, 'Can we go home now? I want to play with my toy soldiers.'

Amelie turned around and went over to him. 'Of course we can,' she said quietly.

Was she right to be concerned about Gage's relationship with the registrar? It could be entirely innocent, couldn't it? Only they seemed so close, so familiar with each other, so much more than just friends.

She glanced back at Gage and said, 'Perhaps we should go home now?'

He inclined his head almost imperceptibly, agreeing with her, acting as though everything was normal. His eyes, though, told a different story. They told her that he had picked up on the atmosphere of unease. He knew that something was wrong.

'If that's what you want,' he murmured, then frowned. 'Have I done something to upset you?'

She shook her head. 'No. I just think that it's time for us to go.'

His gaze narrowed on her. 'Is this because of Lewis?' he asked. 'Is that why you've suddenly backed away from me...because you feel a sense of loyalty to him?'

'I don't know what you mean,' she said. Why was he asking her about Lewis? What did he have to do with anything?

'You don't?' His mouth made a straight line. 'All right, if that's the way you feel. I understand if you don't want to talk about it. Perhaps you're right. I should never have made a move on you in the first place. It was the wrong thing to do.' He picked up his car keys. 'Come on, then. We should get your boy home.'

Her boy? She gazed at him in bewilderment. He had said that once before, hadn't he? A frown crept into her eyes. Had she guessed right in the first place. Did he actually think that Connor was her son?

Her mind was spinning. He must believe, then, that Lewis was his father. The extent of what had happened hit her full force. He must have thought all along that she was a single parent, and that she and Lewis had some kind of agreement over the mutual care of their child.

Amelie stared at him. She ought to tell him the truth, here and now, hadn't she, but something in her held her back from doing that. Wasn't it for the best that she should let him go on thinking that way? She needed a barrier between them, a way of making him keep his distance, because she was deeply reluctant to get involved. That would only lead to heartache and despair, wouldn't it, and hadn't she experienced enough of that already in her life?

Perhaps she would delay putting him right on that score for the time being. That, surely, would give her peace of mind?

CHAPTER EIGHT

GAGE drove them back to Amelie's cottage, and just as she was helping Connor from the car, she saw another driver pull up at the kerb.

'It looks as though I timed that just right,' Lewis said, locking up and coming over to them. 'I was hoping to see you, Amelie.' He glanced at Gage, inclining his head towards him in acknowledgement. Gage returned the greeting in similar vein, his expression closed.

'Were you? Have you just come from work?'

'Yes.' He lowered his voice so that Connor wouldn't hear. 'I've brought Rags home with me. I thought Connor might like to play with him for a bit, but I wanted to ask you if it was all right first.'

Amelie smiled. 'I'm sure he'd love that.'

'Good. I have him in a box in the car. I'll go and fetch him.'

'Do you want to take Connor with you? I'm sure he'd love to help.' She turned to Connor. 'Do you want to go and see the puppy? He's in the car.'

Connor's face lit up like a beacon, and Lewis looked over at Amelie and said with a smile, 'I guess we'll be back in a minute or two.'

She watched him go, and then looked awkwardly at Gage. He probably didn't know that Lewis lived next door to her, and he must imagine that he had turned up especially to see her.

'His mouth is healing up well after the bite, don't you think?' she said.

He nodded. 'Yes, it is. The surgeon made a good job of the sutures.' His manner was taut, and she knew that he must still be thinking of what had happened between them at his house.

Was she doing the right thing in keeping the truth from him? She was beginning to have second thoughts about her decision, but just then Connor came back towards her, with Lewis following close behind. He was cradling the puppy in his arms, a small bundle of golden fur, with silky ears and big brown eyes.

'Look at him,' he exclaimed. 'Isn't he lovely?'

'He's beautiful,' Amelie murmured, reaching down to stroke the pup.

'He's not allowed to go out for walks yet,' Connor said. 'He has to have his 'jections first, but when he's old enough I can take him out on the lead.'

Gage ran a finger lightly over the puppy's fur. 'That's going to be something to look forward to, isn't it?' he said with a smile. A moment later, he straightened up. 'I should go,' he said.

'Oh…OK,' Amelie murmured. She wasn't sure that she wanted him to go just yet, but she added, 'I expect we've kept you long enough, and I suppose I'd better get Connor inside. Thanks for taking us to the beach. We had a lovely time.'

He nodded. 'You're welcome.' He was frowning as he

walked over to his car, and Amelie watched him go and
wanted to run after him. He had kissed her and set her
soul on fire, and her nervous system was still in a state
of total chaos. She was shaken up by what had happened
and she wasn't sure that she would ever recover.

Life had to go on, though, and at work next day she
looked in on Nathan and then went to find her first patient.
She wanted to keep busy, to drive everything from her
mind and so she worked steadily throughout the morning.

If she could have avoided Gage she would have, but
he was there beside her as she attended to a woman with
a heart disorder.

'We'll give her oxygen and obtain intravenous
access,' he said, checking the heart monitor. 'I'm going
to start with a bolus of adenosine to see if we can bring
the heart rate down.'

Some time later, Amelie said quietly, 'It seems to be
working. Are you going to give her esmolol?'

He nodded. 'We'll do it by infusion.'

When their patient was stabilised, they walked back
to the desk and Gage wrote up the woman's chart.
'Didn't you say that Connor's grandmother has a similar
complaint?' he asked. 'How is she doing?'

'She's beginning to feel better, by all accounts.' The
nursery teacher had spoken to Emma on the phone the
other day and relayed the news to her. 'She has some
problems with the node that regulates the heart rate. It's
been acting up and causing a gallop rhythm, so that
she's been struggling to cope. It makes her feel faint and
breathless, but the doctor has given her some beta
blockers, and things are calming down at last.'

She wished that she could get in touch with Emma

to tell her about Nathan, but so far that had proved difficult. There must be something wrong with Emma's mobile phone, and there was no phone at the holiday cottage, so all she could do was ask the nursery school and day care to relay the news to her.

'That's good, isn't it? Sometimes, if these conditions don't calm down, we have to do a cardioversion to put things right, but she's done well to avoid that.' He glanced at her. 'Are you about to go off for your lunch-break just now? Because I wondered if we could perhaps go together.'

She nodded. 'I was planning on going to the staff restaurant after I've been up to see Nathan.'

'Shall I meet up with you in half an hour, say? I could order for you if you let me know what you want.'

'Yes, if you like.' It wouldn't do any harm to have lunch with him, would it? She had to go on working with him, and somehow they had to find a way of making it go smoothly. Much as she might hope that he had come to care for her, and her alone, she wasn't going to kid herself on that score. He might have kissed her, but that didn't have to mean anything.

When she went into the restaurant some time later, she found that he had already picked out a table for them. He had ordered the cheese salad she had asked for, and there was ice cream and fruit to follow.

'How is Nathan?' Gage asked, as she sat down opposite him. 'Has there been any change?'

She shook her head. 'He's no better, and I'm beginning to be really scared for his chances. He's on dialysis to preserve his kidney function, and I don't know what to do. I feel so helpless.'

'I'm sorry, Amelie.'

She grimaced. 'It doesn't look good, and it doesn't help that he's still agitated about his problems at work. He wanted to be a vet, but he thinks that's all gone by the board now.'

'At least he's focussing on getting out of here.'

'I'm not so sure about that. He seems delirious a lot of the time. It just comes out in snatches of conversation.' She dipped her fork into the grated cheese. 'He was offered a place at college, but he needs to be able to go on working at the rescue centre part time to keep him in funds.'

'It would be a real blow, wouldn't it, if he lost his job?' Gage said, frowning.

She toyed with her salad. 'That's true, but I hope it won't come to that.' She sent Gage a quick glance. 'Apparently the boss agreed that it would be a good idea to have video surveillance, but they haven't had any trouble over the last day or so. I'm just wondering if that's because some of the animals have been moved to different quarters. Perhaps they aren't so easy to get at now, or whoever is responsible for letting them out might be finding it too much trouble. That could be the reason that it hasn't occurred since Nathan's been away.'

Gage frowned. 'It actually sounds more like the work of children than anyone out to cause major damage.'

'That's true, except that the outer doors were still locked. It's all been very odd.' She was thoughtful for a moment. 'Some of the floors were resurfaced, but as soon as they dry out, the animals will be returned to their original housing.'

She finished off her salad and put her plate to one

side. Gage was eating something more substantial, a shepherd's pie with vegetables, and she said lightly, 'You look as though you needed that.'

He nodded. 'I burn up a lot of energy.'

Her mouth curved. 'It was generous of you to take us out yesterday, Connor and me. I think there was enough food to feed an army. You certainly pack a good picnic.'

'I was hoping that you would enjoy it.'

'I did.' She was wistful for a second or two. 'The last time I went on a picnic was when I'd just qualified as a doctor. Nathan and I went for a day out with some friends and celebrated with a picnic by the lake. He was so proud that I had managed to get through medical school.' She smiled. 'It was summertime, and he said that we should have a feast of strawberries and cream and champagne.' Her eyes were sad. 'It's hard to believe that he's in such a bad way now.'

Gage reached for her across the table, his hands holding hers in a gentle clasp. 'You have to hold on to the thought that he'll get through this,' he murmured. 'I know things look bad right now, but you have to try to be positive.'

'I know. I know what you're saying is true, but it's hard.'

'You're not alone in this,' he murmured. 'I'm here with you, and you can count on me. I hope you realise that.'

'Maybe.' She straightened and he released her hand.

'You know,' he said, 'you do have family to call on as well, if you could bring yourself to do that. Have you thought any more about getting in touch with your father? I know that you don't want to, but in years to come you might regret that you didn't take the opportunity.'

'Why would I do that? You know how I feel about him.'

His mouth flattened. 'You said that Nathan thought the world of him to begin with, and perhaps underneath all the hurt those feelings have never really gone away. It could be that knowing that his father has taken the trouble to come to see him will give him the extra boost that's needed to help him to pull through. Sometimes it isn't medicine alone that's important. We need to know that the people who matter most to us are close by.'

'You think I'm being selfish, don't you?' She shook her head. 'That's unfair. You don't have any idea how much he hurt us.'

'I know that it must have been terrible for you. I just wonder if he was really bad all through, as bad as you seem to think. He must have some redeeming qualities surely?'

She gave a strange little smile. 'My mother had faith in him. She loved him, and even though she was broken-hearted when he left, she always held on to that small part of her that believed he would come back one day. No other relationship was quite the same for her, even though she met other men who cared for her after he had gone.'

Her mouth straightened. 'Perhaps he knew that and became jealous and wondered if he had made a mistake in leaving. He did come back, from time to time, just at the right moment to mess things up for her.' She grimaced. 'There was one time when he phoned her up and said that he wanted to try to make a go of things again. She told us about it, and she said he sounded so sincere. He wanted to meet her and talk about a recon-ciliation, but we didn't want her to go. We thought, Nathan and I, that it would be the same as every other time he'd thought about coming home. We didn't want her to be devastated when he changed his mind later on.'

She stopped speaking, averting her face from him, and Gage put out a hand to touch her arm. 'When was this? Was it a long time ago?'

'It was some five or six years ago.' She looked back at him. 'I was at medical school, and Nathan was just about to start his first job after leaving college. My mother was living her own life, getting on with things, and we didn't really have any right to tell her to not go. In the end we said that it was up to her, and that only she could make the decision whether to go through it all again, but we were afraid for her. We wanted her to be happy.'

'So she went to meet him?'

'Yes. They were going to have dinner together at a restaurant in the town, and he was coming in from another city where he was working at the time. They decided to meet up at the restaurant...' Her voice faltered. 'Only my mother didn't make it because she was involved in a head-on crash with someone who overtook on a bend in the road. She didn't survive.'

He pulled in a sharp breath. 'That must have been terrible for you. I think I understand, now, why you don't want to have anything to do with him. Every memory you have of him must be tinged with hurt.'

'That's pretty much how it is. Even though that wasn't his fault, it still hurts to know that she might still be alive if she hadn't gone to meet him. Time doesn't seem to make it any less painful, but perhaps that will change.'

'I hope so, otherwise you're going to be carrying around too much of a burden for too long. You need to be able to let it go at some point.'

'I know.' She glanced at her watch and gave a small sigh. 'I should be getting back to work.' She stood up and prepared to leave.

He nodded. 'I should go, too,' he said, getting to his feet and walking with her to the door. 'I have to prepare for the course I'm attending, and there's still some packing that I have to do.'

Amelie had almost forgotten about the course. She had expected it to be some time in the future, and she was surprised that he was packing for it already. 'When do you go?'

'I'm driving over there later this afternoon.'

'Today?' It was a bolt from out of the blue and her nerves juddered in response. He was going so soon? 'Oh, I see... I didn't realise that.'

She tried to say it calmly, but the news had hit her hard, and it came to her in a shock wave of revelation that she really didn't want him to go. She had made the mistake of coming to care for him in a big way, and she needed him to be with her. He had been gentle and considerate, kind and supportive, and the plain truth was... she loved him. She didn't want him to go anywhere, not even for a few days.

She was subdued as they walked out into the corridor. 'I hope it goes well for you.'

'Thanks.' They turned into an empty stairwell. 'I'll go down here and out to the car park, if you're going straight back to A and E.'

She nodded, and Gage was about to go down the stairs when he suddenly swivelled around and looked at her searchingly. Then, as though he was acting on the spur of the moment, he pulled her to him and kissed her briefly, a swift, demanding kiss that took her breath away and left her senses in uproar. Her blood was surging through her veins, rampaging through every part of her as though she was being taken by storm.

He dragged his mouth from hers and looked into her eyes. 'Goodbye, Amelie,' he said. 'Take care.'

Just as suddenly as he had turned towards her, he broke away and left her, taking the stairs as though the wind was at his heels.

She stared after him. Her lips were tingling with the sheer exhilaration of those stolen moments and her mind was in turmoil.

All her doubts came rushing back in full force. He was going away for two whole days and she didn't have the first idea how she was going to cope. She had grown so used to having him around, but now he wouldn't be there when she most needed him. What was she thinking of, letting him into her heart?

She went back to work. Even after she had finished for the day, the knowledge that he had gone weighed heavily on her.

There were no answers waiting for her at work the next day either. For the first time since she had started work in A and E she couldn't turn to Gage, and she felt lost and alone as though the worries of the world had settled on her shoulders.

Her brother's condition was giving cause for concern and she wished that there was something she could do to help him. She stared at the notice-board by the coffee-machine where her father's business number was pinned up, and scanned the details once more.

Was Gage right when he said that if Nathan could see

his father it might aid his recovery? Was she being selfish by holding back?

Her whole being rebelled against getting in touch with him, but she didn't know what to do for the best. She thought about it some more and came to a decision, and before she could change her mind, she went over to the desk and called her father's office.

It came as a dampener to hear that he wasn't in, but she left a message with the secretary and hoped that he would return her call. Then she went to find her patient.

'Mr Bryant was walking his dog,' Chloe said, 'and when the dog fell into an old mineshaft, he tried to go after him to pull him out. As a result, he wrenched his knee rather badly.'

Amelie looked at the man in concern. 'It does look very swollen,' she said, examining the limb. 'Can you extend your knee at all?'

He tried, but then shook his head. 'It's too painful. What do you think I've done to it?'

'It's hard to tell at the moment. We'll need to get X-rays done in order to be certain, but I think you could have fractured the kneecap, and it looks as though there's been a seepage of blood into the joint. That's probably what's causing the swelling to be so tense and painful.' She looked at him. 'May I ask—how did the dog come out of all this?'

The man made a face. 'Oh, he's fine, the wretch. I fell and then wrenched my knee, trying to make a grab for him, and he scrambled out and ran off, happy as you please. At least he came back later, and stayed with me until help came. Would you believe it…there isn't even a scratch on him.'

Amelie laughed. 'And this is what you get for your trouble? It just isn't fair, is it?' She bent to examine his knee once more. 'I'm going to immobilise it in a backslab while we get the films done, and then I'll take another look at you. I'll most likely need to get an orthopaedic appraisal, and that could mean that you'll need to go to Theatre in order to have things put right. The surgeon will probably need to realign the kneecap and draw fluid off the knee.' She turned to Chloe. 'Let's give him something for the pain in the meantime.'

They moved away from the bedside and Amelie wrote up the medication on the man's chart. 'Is there any news of what happened to my renal patient—the woman whose children were asking to see her? I asked for a consultation, and the last I heard she was being taken to the renal unit.'

Chloe nodded. 'She seems to be responding to treatment. She was put on dialysis last night, apparently, and the infection is gradually being brought under control.'

Amelie breathed a sigh of relief. 'That's good to hear. I was really worried about her.'

'I know you were.'

Somehow, Amelie managed to get through the rest of the day. She hadn't realised how lonely she would be without Gage around to share the smallest everyday happening with her. She wanted to talk to him, to be with him, and now that he wasn't there she was utterly miserable.

When she finally finished her shift and went to pick up Connor from day care, she was tired and more than a little unhappy, but she tried to put on a brave face for the child.

'Have you had a good day?' she asked him.

'Yes, we made leaf print pictures and it was fun. I got paint all over my hands.' He waved the finished picture under her nose.

'That's lovely. You managed to put at least some of the paint on the paper, I see.' Amelie smiled.

'Yes, and my mummy called. She says she's coming home to see me and daddy.'

'Did she? That's good news, isn't it?' Amelie was filled with a sudden feeling of relief, and just as she was looking around for the teacher, the woman came and found her. 'Go and put your coat on, Connor,' Amelie said, 'and we'll hurry back home.'

He skipped away to get his coat and change out of his indoor shoes.

'I see Connor must have told you about the phone call,' the teacher said. 'His mother rang at lunchtime and when we told her what had happened she said that she would start out for home almost immediately. She had to make a few arrangements, she said, and she was going to bring her mother with her, so she wasn't exactly sure when she would get back. She thought it would be some-where around six o'clock, and she said that she would come over to your house to see Connor first of all.'

'Oh, thank you for sorting all that out for me. It's such a relief. I've been worrying about it for ages. All my attempts to get in touch with her so far have come to nothing.'

'I think part of the problem was that her phone was out of order and the phone at the house had been dis-connected. She had to use a pay phone to call us.'

'I wondered if it was something like that. Anyway,

it's wonderful news that she's coming home. Thanks for passing the message on.'

'You're welcome.' The woman smiled and said goodbye to Connor as he came back to Amelie's side.

They hurried out to the car park and headed for home. 'I'll make tea, and then I expect you can play with the puppy for a while,' Amelie said. 'Lewis has to go out for a while, and he asked if we could look after him.'

Connor gave her a beaming smile. 'This is my very best day,' he said.

'I know.' She lightly ruffled his hair.

Amelie wasn't so sure about the day being so good when a couple of hours had gone past and Emma still hadn't arrived.

'When will Mummy be home?' Connor asked.

'I'm not quite sure,' Amelie said. 'It depends on how long it takes her to drive back.' She didn't want to give him any false hopes. He was already disappointed that she hadn't arrived, and he would be watching the clock and asking every few minutes when she was going to be there.

He frowned, sensing trouble. 'Will I be in bed when she gets home?'

'Well, it's already past your bedtime now. We might have to think about getting you settled down in a little while because it's late, and you need to rest.'

His lip jutted. 'I don't want to go to sleep.'

'I know, and I'll let you stay up a little longer…but if you should fall asleep, I'll wake you up and let you know when she's gets here. Would that make you feel better?'

He thought about it. 'Do you promise?'

'I promise.'

In the end, he fell asleep on the settee, and Amelie

carried him up to bed. She was getting worried now, because there was still no sign of Emma, and it wasn't like her to let Connor down. Could she have gone to the hospital first, or dropped her mother off at her own house and been delayed there?

She checked up on both of those options, but neither of them bore fruit.

'I haven't seen them,' Connor's grandfather said. 'My wife phoned me and said she was coming home, but she hasn't arrived and I was beginning to worry. Do you think they might have stopped off on the way to get something to eat?'

'It's possible, I suppose.' She didn't think it was very likely, but something might have happened to cause them to do that. It could be that Emma's mother had felt unwell. 'I'll see if I can find out what's happening,' she told him, 'and as soon as I have any news, I'll get back to you.'

'Thanks, I appreciate that. I'll do the same.'

Amelie stared down at the phone after she had cut the call. Despite what she had said to Emma's father, she was seriously concerned. It was very late, and she had a horrible feeling that something was wrong, and she didn't know what to do about it. Wouldn't Emma have been in touch with them if she knew that they were waiting for her to come home?

Amelie's nerves were raw. If only Gage could have been with her. He would have known what to do. He was always calm and clear-headed, and just hearing his voice would make her feel that everything was all right once more.

Was it possible that she could talk to him? Couldn't she just ring the hotel where he was staying and share her troubles with him? He had said that he would always be there for her, hadn't he?

Suddenly a little ray of hope grew in her, and she quickly found the number of the hotel and asked if she could be put through to him.

'I'll try his room for you,' the receptionist said. 'Would you hold for a moment, please?'

Amelie waited, nervous excitement jangling inside her. What would he make of her calling him at this hour? Would he mind?

'Hello.'

It wasn't Gage who answered and Amelie went into shock. It was a woman's voice and she didn't sound at all like the receptionist. Had she been put through to the wrong room?

Confused, Amelie said, 'I wondered if I could speak to Dr Bracken? Dr Gage Bracken. Is he there?'

'I'm afraid he's not able to come to the phone just at the moment,' the woman said, and all at once Amelie recognised the voice. Her heart seemed to stop beating for a moment or two. 'Can I pass a message on? I'm his colleague, Gina.'

'I…I don't think so…' Amelie felt sick, and her mind was whirling. What was Gina doing in his room, answering his phone?

'Are you sure?'

'I'm sure. It doesn't matter. I'll leave it.'

Amelie put the receiver down and broke off the call. She was trembling, her whole body recoiling from the shock of finding that he was closeted in his hotel room with the registrar.

Why had she ever thought that he might be there for her

when she needed him? All this time, while she had been thinking about him, he had been with another woman. All his soft, caring words and passionate kisses had been no more than empty gestures. They had meant nothing.

She was right not to have put her trust in him, wasn't she? But the damage was done all the same. She had let herself fall in love with a man who would never be there for her, and who could never be relied on. In the end, hadn't she made the very same mistake that her mother had made all those years ago?

CHAPTER NINE

'ARE you sure you don't mind doing this for me, Lewis?' Amelie looked at him worriedly. 'I hate to keep imposing on you this way, but I don't know what else to do.'

'It's all right. I'll stay here and keep an eye on Connor for you. It's no problem, really. I doubt he'll wake up until morning now that he's tucked up in bed. I'll put my feet up on the settee and watch television for a while.' He glanced at the puppy snoozing in the wash basket in a corner of the kitchen and gave a wry smile. 'I don't mind at all, honestly, and, besides, Rags seems to have made himself at home. I think he's down for the night and I don't have the heart to move him.'

'He does look cosy, doesn't he?' She breathed a sigh of relief. 'You're an angel, you know that, don't you?' Studying him briefly, she tried to gauge his mood. 'How did your evening go? Did you meet your girlfriend? I must say, I wasn't expecting you to come home quite so early.'

'Yes, and it was great. She's been away on a trip…part of her college course…and she managed to get the afternoon and evening off, which was fantastic for us, but she has to drive back to the campus tonight.

There's a meeting of the students' union first thing tomorrow morning, and she's the chairperson.'

Amelie winced. 'It must be difficult for both of you, with Jenny away at college and you working back here.'

He shrugged. 'It won't be for too much longer. This is her final year, and we've managed to see each other most weekends up to now. She's a great girl. I know I've made the right choice.'

'She's not done so badly herself.'

Lewis smiled. 'I expect you're biased because I'm your brother's best friend.' Then he sobered. 'Are you sure that you want to make this journey? It might be for nothing and, then again, you can't be sure what you might be up against. The weather forecast says there's mist coming down over the moor. It isn't going to be a pleasant drive.'

'I know that, but I have to go and make sure that Emma hasn't met with an accident or broken down somewhere. It said on the news that there had been some sort of incident on the main road across the moor, involving several cars. It was supposed to have happened some time after five o'clock, and I don't like the sound of that time frame. From what I could see of the TV footage, it didn't look as though Emma's car was involved, but she would have been driving home that way about that time. It might have been that she was delayed because of it somehow, but I won't rest easily unless I go and see for myself.'

'I would have thought the fallout from the accident would all have been dealt with by now, wouldn't you? It's late, and surely any people involved would have been taken to hospital?'

'I don't know. The news programme said they had to bring in lifting gear to move vehicles out of the way, and, anyway, I've checked with the hospitals. Emma hasn't been brought in, and neither has her mother.'

Lewis grimaced. 'Make sure you let me know what's happening, won't you? I don't want to have to worry about you as well as Nathan.'

'I'll ring you as soon as I get the chance, I promise.' She checked her bag and prepared to stow everything in the car. She had gathered together a couple of blankets, just in case, a torch, and her medical bag. 'Do you think there's anything I've forgotten?'

He nodded. 'A hot drink. I made a Thermos of coffee for you and left it on the worktop by the kettle.' He waved a hand towards it. 'It can be cold out there this late at night, and your car's heater isn't all that brilliant.'

'Thanks, Lewis. I'll grab it on my way out.'

She left the house a few minutes later, after checking the map for the route she was about to take. Emma would have been coming in the opposite direction, of course, and it would be difficult for Amelie to examine every part of the road, especially on the outgoing journey. Nevertheless, she wouldn't be content until she had made the attempt. If Emma had been involved in an accident, every hour could count.

Amelie hadn't been on the road for more than half an hour before she realised that Lewis had been right about the journey. It was dark and cold, and the mist was beginning to close in, swirling towards her in patchy wisps that suddenly became dense and made it difficult to see the road ahead. If only Gage was there beside her. Things would seem so much brighter if he was with her.

She crushed the thought as swiftly as it had emerged. There was no point in thinking about him, or in wishing for what was never going to happen. He wasn't ever going to be with her in the way that she wanted, was he? In fact, he was cosy and warm in his hotel room, and he had company to keep him entertained, didn't he?

Her fingers tightened on the steering-wheel. She would not think about that. Gage was her boss and from now on she would think only of him as someone she worked with. She would keep her emotions firmly grounded, and treat him as though he was just another colleague. That way she could at least cling on to her self-respect and not sink into a bottomless well of thinking about what might have been.

'I'm here for you,' he had said. 'You can count on me.' But it wasn't true, was it? He was as unreliable as her father and she wouldn't let him fool her into thinking otherwise ever again.

She made an effort to concentrate her attention on the road ahead, looking out for anything untoward, anything that might give her a clue as to what could have happened to Emma.

When she came towards the site of the accident on the opposite side of the road, she drove to the intersection further on and turned the car around, coming back along the route that Emma would have taken.

Floodlights had been put in place to facilitate the rescue process. The emergency vehicles were still in attendance, police, a fire engine and ambulances, along with a tow truck. Amelie drew her car to a halt some short distance away, pulling in to a convenient lay-by.

She collected her medical bag, then stepped out of

the car and went over to the police officer who was overseeing operations. 'I'm a doctor,' she said. 'Can I be of any help?'

'I'll find out for you,' he answered. 'I think the ambulance crew have things under control, but they may be glad of another pair of hands.'

She went with him to where the paramedics were transferring patients to one of the ambulances. 'We're OK here,' the ambulance driver said. 'We've accounted for everyone and they're all being attended to. There weren't any fatalities, but we've had to deal with several crush injuries and broken limbs. It actually could have been much worse.'

'Among the injured, did you see a young woman with light brown hair, about twenty-five years old, who was travelling with an older woman? I've been looking for my friend, Emma Tyler, and her mother. They were supposed to be driving this way some hours ago, and I haven't heard from them yet. I'm worried that they might have been caught up in the accident.'

The man frowned and shook his head. 'We haven't treated anyone of that description. In fact, you're the second one to ask me that, tonight. Another doctor was enquiring about them, just a few minutes ago.'

Amelie frowned. Another doctor? That was more than a coincidence, surely? Who would know about Emma and her mother, apart from herself? And who could this doctor be?

He indicated an ambulance some distance away. 'He's over there, lending a hand with the last of the injured people. He might be able to help you out.'

'I'll go and talk to him,' she said. 'Thanks.'

She made her way over to the other ambulance and carefully looked around. One of the paramedics was closing the ambulance doors, while another was talking to someone.

Amelie came to a sudden halt. Even in the darkness, she recognised that tall, familiar figure. But wasn't he supposed to be at the conference hotel? What was Gage doing there?

She floundered for a moment, and then she pulled herself together and went over to him. His face was shadowed in the darkness. 'I didn't imagine for one minute that I would find you here,' she said huskily. 'I thought you were at the hotel.'

'I was.' He reached for her, as though reassuring himself that it was really her. Amelie stiffened. Seeing him here had set her heart pounding, but she was wary of believing in him in any way, and she certainly couldn't trust her own judgement.

Sensing that something wasn't quite right, he looked at her oddly. His brows drew together in a dark line, and he let his hands drop to his sides. 'You're right, I was at the hotel, but Gina told me that you called. At least, she didn't recognise the voice, so I checked up.'

'Did you?' She was surprised that he had gone to the trouble of doing that. Had she caught him unawares?

He nodded. 'I realised that it must have been you, so I rang your home number and Lewis told me what was happening and that you were on your way out here. I was concerned for you. I guessed that you wouldn't have called me unless you were upset or troubled.'

'Even so, I wouldn't have expected you to come out here. I just...' She broke off. She hadn't thought beyond actually being able to talk to him, and then everything had gone wrong, and now she felt constrained by events, so that she couldn't explain to him what was going through her mind.

'I wanted to do whatever I could to help, so I drove along the route that Emma would have been taking. I hoped I might see something that would give us a clue as to what might have happened.' He studied her cautiously. 'I told you that I would be there for you, if you needed me.'

'Yes, but I didn't realise that you would be with Gina. I wouldn't have rung if I'd known that. I mean, I knew that you were attending the course together, but I hadn't realised that I would be intruding on you both.'

She clamped her mouth shut, unwilling to dig herself any deeper into the hole she had made for herself. It wouldn't do her any good at all to lay her feelings bare, would it?

He was looking at her in a faintly puzzled fashion and she guessed he must think she was rambling. He didn't feel the same way about her, and why would he make any sense of what she was saying? Perhaps he was simply uncomfortable because she had discovered he had been with Gina and he wanted to make amends. He didn't owe her anything at all, though. He hadn't made any promises of undying love, had he?

She looked around, trying to take in her surroundings. In the darkness the moor was bleak, and a chill wind was blowing across the desolate landscape. Of course, he must have driven across the moor to get to the hotel in the first place. She'd forgotten that this was his route home.

'I can't think what could have happened to them,' she said. 'The ambulance driver told me they hadn't been found. Perhaps I've come on a wild-goose chase.'

'I'm not so sure about that. I've been taking a look around, and it looks as though there are skid marks further back along the road, and the verge shows some faint signs of tyre marks where the grass has given way to mud. There's no sign of a vehicle, but I'm just wondering if someone could have swerved off the road somewhere along here.'

'You mean that Emma might have been caught up in all this after all?'

'It's possible. It was a bit chaotic, apparently, with one vehicle swerving over the central reservation and going across the path of the oncoming cars. It could have been that the visibility was bad at that point, though it seems to have cleared now. It may be that another car might have been caught up in the mêlée and was shunted down the embankment. I was just about to go and take a look.'

'I'll go with you.'

'OK, but I'd better go and tell the fire chief what we're doing. They've about finished here, but we might find that we need help later. I'll see if I can get them to hold off leaving for a while.'

As soon as he had done that, he took her to where the turf of the embankment had been churned up and the low-lying vegetation had been flattened. It was difficult to make out any skid marks, but Gage led the way, shining his torch ahead of them to light up their path. Amelie made her way cautiously over the uneven ground.

'Watch your step,' Gage said. 'It's a bit marshy around

here.' The land sloped down to a wide ditch, which was overgrown with brambles and a thick hedgerow.

Amelie stumbled, and he reached for her hand and guided her the rest of the way. 'It's hard to make out anything in this gloom,' he said. He flashed the wide beam of the torch all around. 'Can you see anything?'

She shook her head. His fingers gripped hers firmly, the muscled tension in his arm lending her powerful support as they ventured further down into the ditch.

'Wait a minute.' She suddenly stopped and he turned to look back at her.

'What is it?'

'I thought I heard something, but it's difficult to make out with all the traffic noise.'

They both fell silent, listening. The wind made an eerie noise, whistling all around them, but through it came an odd little sound.

'It's coming from over there,' Gage said. 'I can see a shape that doesn't seem to belong…a dark out-line…but I can't quite make it out.'

They moved towards the shadows, and after a moment or two Amelie gave a sudden gasp. 'It's a car,' she said. 'It looks as though it has somehow veered partly onto its side.'

'I'll go and take a look,' Gage murmured. 'Perhaps you should stay there, while I go and see if there's anyone inside.'

He was protecting her, asking her to keep back in case there was something she wouldn't want to see, but Amelie ignored his request and went with him. She peered inside the car as Gage shone the torch all around, and the breath snagged in her throat.

'They're in there,' she said. She could see two women, their faces pale in the moonlight. They weren't moving. Fearful, she felt for the handle of the car door and tried to pull it open, but it wouldn't budge. 'It's stuck. I can't do it.' There was a rising note of desperation in her voice. 'I think the metal must have warped in the smash.'

'Let me try,' Gage said, coming to stand beside her. He worked on it for some time, trying the doorhandle, tugging and heaving with all his might, using his foot as a lever in order to release the catch, but still it wouldn't give.

'It's stuck fast. I'll have to try to wrench it open,' he muttered. 'If I can get the boot open, there might be something in there that I can use, or we could even gain access that way. Luckily it's a hatchback, so that should make things easier.' He shone the torch inside the vehicle once more, and Amelie sucked in a breath.

Emma made a frail movement. She lifted a hand and pressed her palm against the window. 'I can't get out,' she mouthed. Amelie strained to hear what she was saying. 'My foot's trapped and I can't undo the window or open the door.' She seemed to shudder. 'I'm so cold.'

'We'll get you out,' Gage promised her. 'How's your mother doing? Is she conscious?' They could both see that the older woman still wasn't moving.

'Yes, but she's not doing too well.'

'All right. Don't worry. We'll get to you both in a minute or two. Can you reach the boot release switch? Does it work?'

Emma nodded, and fumbled for the centre console, while Gage went around to the back of the car and pulled at the lid of the boot. It swung open and he scrabbled around in there for a time. Then he came back to the door, armed with a tool of some sort.

'I'm going to use this as a lever to try to wrench the door open,' he told Amelie and Emma. He put the bar into position against the door and the bodywork of the car and then applied pressure, so that within a moment or two the catch gave way. Amelie heaved a thankful sigh.

'Are you hurt at all?' she asked Emma. She could see that Emma had a nasty gash on her forehead, but she was conscious and lucid, and Amelie wasn't too worried about that for the moment.

'My foot's throbbing a bit,' Emma said. 'I've been trying to free it, but it's caught between the foot pedals and the side of the car. I think it must be swollen and the car's wing has been pushed inwards down there.' She was shivering, and Gage took off his jacket and wrapped it around her.

'I'm going to climb in through the back and take a look at your mother,' he said. 'I can't get around to the other side and it will be easier than trying to reach over from your side. Has she been unconscious at all?'

'I think we were both out for a time. She's breathing, and I don't think she has any major injuries, as far as I can tell, but her heart rate is causing her problems. I think she should have had another tablet before now, but they're in her bag, and that's been thrown in the back somewhere.' Emma's face crumpled. 'I feel so useless, not being able to get out of here or do anything,' she said, her voice trailing away on a note of frustration.

'I'll see if I can find it,' Amelie said, climbing into the back of the car after Gage. She hunted about and retrieved the bag, searching through it for the tablets. She found the foil-wrapped strip of beta-blockers and handed them to Gage. 'How is she?'

'Her pulse is around one-eighty,' he murmured, 'and her breathing is compromised, but apart from that she isn't doing too badly. She has a badly bruised arm, but there are no broken bones as far as I can tell.' He checked the foil strip. 'She's exhausted, but if we give her a double dose of the medication and get her on oxygen therapy, she should start to recover.'

Mrs Tyler wasn't saying anything, but she was aware of what was going on, and their main concern was to lower her heart rate so that her breathing would improve.

Amelie went back to Emma and opened up her medical bag, passing Gage a pack of glucose drink so that Mrs Tyler could wash the tablets down. 'That's good news, but I'm worried about getting them both out of here. Do you think we'll be able to push back the metalwork that's trapping Emma's foot? It looks as though it's badly bruised, but I can't see any major damage.' She gave Emma a couple of painkilling tablets and then started to clean up the wound on her brow.

'I doubt it, because it may be an anti-impact bar that's causing the problem. Mrs Tyler is trapped, too, but that's something to do with the door pinning her back on this side. I'll have a look and see what I can do. Failing that, we should get hold of the fire crew and let them take over.'

Amelie applied a dressing to Emma's wound, while Gage came around to the side of the car to look at the damage. 'We need cutting equipment to get them out of here,' he said. 'Will you stay here with them while I go back to the fire crew?'

'Yes, of course. There are some things in my car that we could do with here...blankets and a Thermos. Would you bring them back with you? Emma and her mother are dehydrated as well as suffering the effects of the cold, and a hot drink will do them both a world of good.'

'I'll do that,' he said, and she handed him her car keys. Then she took off her own jacket and put it around Emma's mother.

Gage hurried away, and Amelie did what she could to help the two women trapped in the car. She climbed into the vehicle from the back and gave Mrs Tyler oxygen with the aid of a bag and mask.

'We should have you out of here before too long,' she told them. 'I know it may not seem that way to you right now, but it looks as though you've both been very lucky. It could have been far worse.'

Emma nodded. 'I know. How did the other drivers come out of it?'

'There weren't any fatalities, according to the ambulance driver.'

Emma let out a slow breath. 'Thank heaven. I didn't really see much of what happened to the other drivers, but I guessed it was bad. I saw the lorry veer over onto my side of the road, and the driver in front tried to swerve to avoid him. Then someone went into him and was spun around and I was caught up at the back. Somehow I ended up being pushed off the road and down the embankment.' She shuddered. 'I was so scared. I was afraid for my mother, and I thought my time was up and I was so worried about what would happen to Connor.'

'He's all right. He was desperate to see you, but he's

tucked up in bed at my house and Lewis is watching over him.'

'That's such a relief.' Emma was quiet for a moment. 'I've been so upset, thinking that we would be here all night, and wondering if anyone would ever find us.'

'You're safe now.' Amelie gently covered her hand with her own. 'You'll see Connor soon enough.'

'And what about Nathan? Tell me about him, please, Amelie. Is he dreadfully ill? Will he get better?' Emma looked grief-stricken, and Amelie tried her best to reassure her.

'I hope so. The medical team are keeping a really close eye on him. I rang the hospital before I came out here, and they say that his condition is much the same. It hasn't worsened, and that has to be good news.'

'Will I be able to go and see him? Will they let me sit with him?'

'I'm sure they will. He'll be so much better for knowing that you're there with him. He hasn't said a lot, but he's been asking for you.'

Emma was silent for a while, and then she said, 'I'm not going to be separated from him again. I don't care what my dad says about it, I want to be with Nathan. He loves me, and he's always wanted us to be a proper couple. He wants us to be married, you know... It's what he's always wanted, but I would never agree because I was worried about what my dad would think. I can't go on this way, though. Nathan is Connor's father, and Connor deserves to be part of a proper family.'

Amelie tried a smile. 'I think you're right.' She glanced at Mrs Tyler, uncertain what she would make of it, but the older woman's expression was relaxed, and now she reached out to pat Emma's hand.

'You do what you feel is best,' Emma's mother said in a thready voice. 'Leave your father to me.'

Emma smiled. 'I can deal with my dad. I've had time to think things through and make up my mind about what's really important. I think I'm a stronger person now. If Nathan gets through this all right, things are going to change.'

Amelie was glad to hear her say that. It warmed her heart to know that Nathan had wanted to do the right thing by Emma all along, and she prayed that he would live to see his dreams realised.

'I need to make some phone calls,' she told the two women. 'I have to tell Lewis what's happening, and then I'll ring Mr Tyler.' She glanced at the older woman. 'Do you want to talk to your husband? Would you be able to manage a few words if I remove the oxygen mask for a while?'

Mrs Tyler nodded. 'He'll be worried about us.' She stopped to steady her breathing as Amelie removed the ventilation mask. 'He's all bluster and hot air, but he's a good man deep down.'

A few minutes later Gage came back with the fire crew, who sized up the situation and tried to work out how they could set about freeing the women from the car. Two paramedics had come along with them, carrying a stretcher.

'I'm glad you're here,' Amelie said, climbing out of the car and going over to them. 'I thought the ambulances would have gone by now.'

'They have. We're from the ambulance car, but when

Dr Bracken said there might be more people who were injured we stayed around in case we were needed.'

'That's good news. Mrs Tyler needs oxygen, and she'll need to go to hospital to be monitored for her heart condition. I think she'll be all right, but she'll probably need to stay overnight for observation. As to Emma, I don't think there are any broken bones, but she should perhaps have the foot X-rayed, and then she may need a support bandage and the use of a crutch for a while.'

The paramedics went to the patients, while Gage went to wrap the blankets around Emma and her mother. He retrieved Amelie's jacket. 'You look frozen,' he said, coming back to her. 'Put it on and then have a hot drink.'

'I will. Thanks.' She watched while both of the women sipped coffee, and then stood back from the car while the firemen got to work with the cutting equipment.

She sent Gage a quick glance. 'I'm really glad that you were here to help out,' she murmured. 'I don't know how I would have managed on my own.'

'I'm sure you would have done extremely well,' he said with a slow smile. 'One way and another, you're turning out to be thoroughly resourceful. You're full of surprises.'

'Am I?' She was doubtful about that.

'Certainly you are. I wouldn't have expected you to go haring off into the countryside late at night, peering into dark corners in search of something you had no idea that you would find. But here you are. I knew as soon as you phoned that there was a problem. I didn't imagine you would be ringing simply to hear my voice.'

She gave a wry smile. That just went to show how little he knew, didn't it? 'What happens now?' she asked.

'Will you be heading back to the hotel?' She held her breath, hardly daring to hope that he might think of abandoning his course and coming back with her.

He started to answer, but just then the firemen called out that they had cut away the first part of the bodywork of the car that was trapping Emma and they were ready to release her from the wreckage.

They both hurried over there, but the paramedics already had things under control. 'We'll take her to the ambulance car,' one of them said, 'and then one of us will come back for her mother.'

Gage was on hand when Mrs Tyler was brought out, and he helped to transfer her to the ambulance car. Amelie collected up the medical bags and the flask and other bits and pieces, and walked with the fire crew back to the lay-by where the cars were parked.

Emma and her mother were in the ambulance car, waiting to be taken to hospital. 'I'll follow you there,' Amelie said, looking in on them.

'Are you sure?' Emma was uncertain. 'I want to stay with my mother until I know that she's all right, but I could perhaps get a taxi back later. I was hoping to be there for Connor when he wakes up.'

'I'll wait with you until we know what's happening,' Amelie told her. 'I'm pretty sure that the medical team will admit your mother overnight, at least, and they may want to keep you there for observation, too, because of your head injury. You shouldn't worry about Connor. I can bring him to see you at the hospital in the morning if things work out that way.'

'Thanks. I suppose you're right. Anyway, I'll feel better knowing that you're with me.'

Amelie looked around for Gage. He was talking to the paramedics a short distance away, but now he turned around and came towards Amelie. 'Are you going straight home?' he asked.

She moved away from the ambulance car and shook her head. 'Not just yet. I'm going over to the hospital first, to make sure that Emma and her mother are going to be all right.'

He frowned. 'Are you going to be safe, driving back? This mist hasn't entirely gone away.'

She nodded. 'The fire crew said that they'll follow me, and the paramedics will be leading the way, so I should be fine.'

'That's good.'

She lifted her gaze to him. More than anything, she wanted him to stay with her, but he wasn't offering to follow her home, was he? It was hard not to let her disappointment show, but perhaps she ought to remember that he had been with Gina before he had come here.

He lifted a hand to her face and lightly brushed her cheek with his thumb. 'You're busy taking care of everyone else, but you look pale and tired, as though someone should be looking after you. I don't like to think of you going back to an empty house.'

'I doubt that will happen.' It was more than likely that Emma would be coming home with her. 'Anyway, Lewis will be there.'

'Ah, yes. I'd forgotten about Lewis.' His mouth made a straight line. 'I don't need to worry about you, then, do I? I thought you and he were living apart, but he's at the house, isn't he?'

'He's looking after Connor for me.' She hesitated, wondering whether she ought to tell him the truth about the situation, but caution won through. 'What will you do?'

'I'll go back to the hotel.'

The air caught in her lungs. Wasn't that what she had known all along? He wouldn't be coming to the hospital with her, and neither was he going to be waiting for her when she arrived home.

He was tender towards her, and caring, but there was nothing more than that, and now that he had done what he could to help her out, he would go back to the place where his heart really belonged.

CHAPTER TEN

'THE doctor said that he wants to keep my mother in hospital overnight for observation, but he doesn't expect any major problems, and she'll probably be able to come home before the day's out,' Emma said, coming into Amelie's kitchen. 'She's so much better already, and they've done a review of her medication and worked out a better dosage for her. My dad's going to meet me at the hospital tomorrow, to see how she's doing and perhaps to bring her back home.'

'How are you going to manage?' Amelie wanted to know. 'You're supposed to be resting that foot, and I don't see much evidence of you doing that so far.'

Emma laughed. 'Well, I do have a crutch to lean on, and at least that means that I can get about. I don't know what on earth Connor's going to make of it.'

Amelie was rueful. 'I told him that I would wake him when you came home, but I feel quite bad about doing that in the early hours of the morning. At least he'll wake up and find you in his room first thing. That will make him happy.'

Emma smiled. 'He's already seen me. I went up and looked in on him while you were making the coffee. I stroked his hair ever so lightly, but he woke up and gave me such a smile. We had a cuddle and I told him we'd go and see his dad first thing in the morning and he went straight back to sleep.'

'That's good. That makes me feel so much better.' Amelie started to tidy up the kitchen. 'I made up a camp bed for you next to his. It's just a fold-away thing with a thin mattress, but the bed is fairly wide. Do you think you'll be all right, sleeping on that?'

'I shall be fine. I'm so tired that even an earthquake wouldn't keep me awake tonight.'

Amelie chuckled. 'You go on up to bed, then. I'll just put these supper dishes in the sink and then I'm turning in myself.'

Emma did as she'd suggested, and Amelie was about to head for the stairs just a few minutes later when the phone rang. She frowned. It couldn't be news of Nathan, could it? She had only seen him an hour or so ago.

He hadn't been asleep when they had been at the hospital, and the nurse had agreed to let them visit for just a few minutes, so she knew he was not doing too badly.

Of course, seeing Emma had made a world of difference to him, and even the nurse thought he looked brighter in himself. The antibiotics seemed to be doing their job at last. What was needed, though, was for him to be able to come off dialysis. That would show that he was finally on the mend.

She picked up the receiver. She was startled to hear Gage's deep voice at the other end of the line, and her heart gave an erratic little tattoo.

'I was just ringing to make sure that you had arrived home safely,' he said, and his gravelly tones curled around her senses and warmed her through and through. 'I didn't want to wake you, if you had already gone to bed. I didn't mean to disturb you and Lewis, but I had to be sure that you were all right.'

A small glow of heat started up inside her. He cared enough to phone and see how she was doing. That had to be good, didn't it?

'I'm fine. Lewis isn't here...he was just helping out. And I was just about to go up to bed, so you didn't wake me. Emma is staying with me, and her mother is in hospital for the night. They say she's going to be all right, and that her heart rate is settling down as they had hoped.'

'That's good news. I'm glad for you.' He was silent for a moment or two and then added in a restrained kind of tone, 'I should go. I'll see you in the morning. 'Night, Amelie.'

He rang off, and Amelie stared down at the receiver. That must have been a slip of the tongue. Surely she wouldn't see him until the day after tomorrow? After all, he would still be at the conference hotel, wouldn't he? Still, things were looking up, if he was taking the trouble to call her.

In the morning Connor was full of beans, jumping about the place and talking ten to the dozen.

'Are we going to see my daddy? Does that mean I don't have to go to school today? Can I stay with you, Mummy? I'll be good, I promise.'

'Yes, to all of that,' Emma said, laughing. 'Hurry up and get ready. Amelie has to be at work soon, and she said that she would drive us over there. Let's not keep her waiting, young man.'

Nathan was much more alert when they went to see him at the hospital just a short time later. He put an arm around Connor and squeezed Emma's hand when she leaned over to kiss him.

'How are you feeling?' Amelie asked.

He gave a faint smile. 'Better for knowing that my family is here,' he said, his glance encompassing all three of them. 'I can't wait to get out of this hospital bed, but I'm still as weak as a kitten.'

'You won't be going very far while you're still attached to that dialysis machine,' Emma commented pithily, 'but you'd better hurry up and make a full recovery, because you have a date to keep—in church.'

Nathan's eyes widened. 'In church?' His voice was frail, as though everything was still an effort for him. 'Does that mean what I think it means?'

Emma nodded. 'You still want me to be Mrs Clarke, don't you?' she asked. 'Or did I get that wrong?'

'You had it right,' he said. 'Definitely.' He frowned. 'But what about your father? I thought you didn't want to upset him?'

'I decided that he was the least of my worries.' Emma smiled. 'Anyway, Mum said she wasn't putting up with his nonsense any longer, and he had better start realising that it was my choice to make, not his.'

Nathan closed his eyes for a second or two, and Amelie guessed that he was trying to gather up his strength. 'I don't want you to fall out with him,' he said. 'He's your father. You need to get on well with him.'

'I know.' Emma leaned over and tenderly stroked his dark hair. 'I've already spoken to him about it, and we've come to a kind of a truce. He said that you've proved yourself by standing by me through all these years since Connor was born, and he knows that I feel the same way about you. He isn't going to cause any trouble for us.' She smiled. 'To be honest, I think it came as a bit of a jolt to him, having Mum go away for a few days. It gave him time to come to his senses. He wants us to be happy and do the right thing.'

Nathan gave a contented sigh. 'That's the best news I've had in a long time.'

A nurse put her head around the door. 'Five more minutes,' she said, 'and then he needs to rest.'

'I'll leave you together for a while,' Amelie said. 'I have to go to work, but I'll see you all later.'

She went to A and E and set about losing herself in her work. Ever since Gage had phoned her, she had been wondering how she was going to adapt to working with him and keeping her feelings remote from him. Could she learn to think of him as just a friend? At least it was easier to do that when he wasn't around.

At lunchtime, though, just as she was filing the last of her patients' charts in a tray on the desk, she was startled to see him walk into the unit, and she stared at him, unable to believe her eyes.

'What are you doing here?' she asked. 'Shouldn't you be some fifty miles away?'

He shook his head. 'I didn't need to stay for the afternoon sessions. I've heard those particular lectures before, and there's no point in repeating them.'

'Won't Gina be wondering why you've left her behind?' The words were out before she could withdraw them, and he looked at her oddly, his dark brows coming together in a frown.

'Why should that matter? She has to complete the course for her assessment. I don't.'

'So she doesn't mind you leaving her?' This was a peculiar arrangement they had, where he would just abandon her and take off as the whim took him. What kind of man would do that?

'Not at all. She seems to be perfectly happy with her colleagues over there.'

'Oh.'

'Oh?' he echoed. 'When you say that, it usually means trouble of some sort. What's the problem?'

Amelie shrugged. 'There's no problem. I just thought she might be put out, that's all, especially after the way you left her to come and help me look for Emma last night.'

'I think you need to explain a little more. I'm not with you... I don't understand what you're getting at.'

Amelie pressed her lips together. 'She was in your room at the hotel, and she answered your phone for you, so I'm assuming that you're more than just colleagues. I just thought she might have trouble accepting that you would just leave her behind as the fancy takes you.'

He tilted his head to one side and studied her. 'I wasn't with Gina. I was in a conference room on the ground floor, having a meeting with one of the professors, and Gina went to my room to fetch a folder for me. I asked the professor to give an opinion on a tricky case I had to deal with, and I'd brought the notes along with me but left them in my room. Gina offered to go and get them for me.'

'Oh,' Amelie said. 'Oh, I see.'

'Do you?' Again, he gave her that sideways look.

'What did you imagine? That she and I were more than just friends?'

Amelie averted her gaze. 'The thought had occurred to me,' she said.

'Hmm. I suppose the hospital grapevine has been bearing fruit.' His glance skimmed over her. 'For a bright, intelligent girl, you can sometimes be very gullible.'

She frowned. 'Do you think so?'

'I do. I most certainly do.' He moved over to the desk and began to flick through the staff rota sheets.

Her mind was reeling. Was he really saying that nothing was going on between him and his registrar? 'I doubt that I'm the only one that jumps to conclusions,' she retorted. 'You seem to be pretty good at doing that yourself.'

His gaze narrowed on her. 'What makes you say that?'

'Well, I somehow had the impression that you thought Connor was my son, and that Lewis might be his father. I don't recall ever telling you that.'

He frowned. 'No, come to think of it, you didn't.' He looked at her steadily. 'Are you saying that it isn't true?'

'It isn't true. Emma is Connor's mother, and Nathan is his father. I was just looking after him while Emma was away. He's my nephew after all.'

His eyes took on an arrested expression. 'I had it all wrong, then. I think Gina said something once about seeing you with the boy...perhaps she simply assumed that he was yours. I didn't question it.'

He put down the papers that he had been holding and came towards her. 'I think we need to talk about this some more. Aren't you supposed to be off duty this afternoon?'

'Yes, it's one of my training days. There was a

tutorial session posted, but the consultant had to cancel.'
She looked at him warily. 'Why? Were you hoping that
I would fill in for someone?'

'No. Actually, I was thinking that you might come
over to my place.'

Her mouth opened and closed. 'Your place?'

'That's what I said.' His grey gaze held a hint of
amusement. 'Am I going to get an answer, or are you
going to stand there looking like a stranded fish for a
while longer?'

'I… Uh…'

She might have found her voice eventually, except that
Chloe came over to her just then and said quickly,
'Amelie, someone's just come in. He's not ill or anything,
so don't worry, but he's asking to see you, and he says
he's your father. He says he knows he should have rung
first, but would you mind him coming to talk to you?'

'My father…' Amelie felt dizzy for a second or two.
'He's here?'

Chloe nodded. 'I showed him through to a waiting
room. I shall have to go. I've a patient waiting.' She sent
Amelie a fleeting glance. 'Are you all right?'

'Yes, I'm fine. Thanks, Chloe. You go and see to
your patient.'

Amelie tried to move, but her legs felt oddly weak
and Gage put out an arm to steady her. 'Did you know
that he was coming in?'

'I wasn't sure. I got in touch with him, but he didn't
call back and I didn't think he was going to turn up.'

Gage gave her a quizzical look. 'That must have
taken some doing. What made you change your mind?'

'You did. I realised that I was being selfish in not

giving him a chance. You were probably right when you said that Nathan would perhaps want to see him, and in the end I wondered if I was trapped in the past and stopping myself from moving on. I couldn't let the troubles of the past colour my future.' She turned to him. 'Does that make sense?'

'It makes a lot of sense.' He smiled at her. 'Are you going to see him? Do you want me to go with you? I won't stay, if you don't want me to.'

'I'll go and see him…and I'd really like you to stay with me. Would you mind?'

'I don't mind at all. I want to do whatever's best for you.'

They went to the waiting room together, and Amelie steeled herself to meet her father. 'Does he know about Nathan's illness?' Gage asked as they approached the door.

'Yes, I told him…or at least, I left the message for him, but Nathan doesn't know that I contacted him. I didn't want to get his hopes up unnecessarily.'

Her father stood up as she went into the room. He was very much as she remembered him, tall and broad shouldered, with brown hair turning grey at the front and at the temples, but there were one or two worry lines that she had not seen before around his eyes and across his forehead.

'Amelie,' he said, coming towards her and reaching for her hands. He clasped her fingers between his palms, holding her with an affection that she remembered from long, long ago.

He looked into her eyes. 'I was hoping that you would get in touch with me. I didn't want to push it, because I know how I've let you down in the past. I want to make up for all that. I realise how badly I behaved, and I'm sorry. I'm really sorry.' His mouth quirked. 'I don't expect you to forgive me. It's enough that you called me, and I hope it can be a new beginning for us.'

'I hope so, too,' she said. She half turned and introduced Gage to him. 'You know each other already, I believe?'

'Yes, that's right. We've done business together... through administrative channels. The hospital uses some of my company's medical equipment.'

She nodded. 'He told me. Gage is very special to me, you know. He saved my life and I'm eternally grateful to him.'

'He saved your life?' Her father shook his head. 'So many things must have happened, and I haven't been here. I don't know how I'm ever going to make it up to you.'

'Perhaps we should just take one day at a time,' she said, 'and make small steps to begin with. If we go slowly and carefully, they might take us where we want to be in the end.'

Gage put an arm around her, his hand resting lightly on her shoulder as if to say, You're doing all right. She slowly began to relax.

They talked for a while, and then she said, 'I'll take you to see Nathan. The nurse rang me a little while ago to say that he's been taken off dialysis. It looks as though the antibiotics are beginning to work, and he's on the mend, but he's still very weak and we'll only be able to stay with him for a short time.'

Her father grimaced. 'I understand. I won't do anything to put his progress back.'

Nathan already had a visitor when they arrived on his ward, and the nurse in charge told them, 'You can stay as long as you don't go tiring him out. I shall come in from time to time and check up on him, to see how he's doing, so mind how you go.'

Amelie nodded. 'We will.'

Lewis was sitting by Nathan's bedside, and Nathan was looking very cheerful as Amelie approached.

'What are you looking so pleased about?' she asked, looking from one to the other. 'No, on second thoughts, tell me in a minute or two. I've brought someone to see you, Nathan.' She stepped aside and let their father come forward. Nathan's face showed a variety of expressions, from shock to pleasure and then curiosity.

'Is this just a flying visit, or are you back in the area permanently?' Nathan asked.

'I'm based here now,' their father said. 'I wanted to move closer to where you both were. I don't want to lose touch again.'

Nathan didn't question his father's sincerity, but somehow Amelie sensed that he didn't need to. Things would be different this time. Their father was not the same man she remembered from her childhood. They seemed to have formed a new understanding of each other, and perhaps over the years their father had come to learn a valuable lesson…that he had to earn his off- spring's respect, and that his life would be the poorer without it.

They talked for a while, and then Amelie said, 'We should go, now— Gage and I. Not you, Dad, or you, Lewis. You stay for as long as the nurse will let you.'

She hesitated, and then asked her brother, 'What was it that was making you look so pleased with yourself when we first came in?'

Nathan grinned. 'Lewis was telling me about the video surveillance at the rescue centre. They put all the animals back where they were before the floors were re-surfaced, and bolted all the doors as usual before bedding them down for the night. When Lewis came in next morning, he found that the dogs were roaming the compound again.'

'Really?' She looked from one to the other of them. 'Did you find out how it happened?'

He nodded. 'It was all on the video tape. Apparently, Buster, the German shepherd, knows a really neat trick. He slides the bolts with his teeth and lifts the latches with his paw. Once he manages to free himself, he goes and helps the others to escape.'

Amelie laughed. 'So you're in the clear? That's great news.'

'It certainly is. I get to keep my job and I'll be able to start my veterinary course once I'm fit and well.'

'That is such a relief.'

'Yes, it is.'

Gage sent him an enquiring look. 'What does Emma feel about you training to be a vet? She looks like the kind of girl who would be supportive.'

'She's pleased about it. Her father is, too. He thinks it's a worthwhile profession.' He frowned. 'We'll struggle a bit to get by, but we'll manage. Lewis and his girlfriend have been through a similar situation, with Jenny away at college and only Lewis earning an income. The difference for Emma and me is that we'll be married and living under one roof, and we'll both have part-time jobs. I don't see too many problems ahead.'

Gage looked startled and glanced quickly at Lewis. 'Your girlfriend's at college? Is she studying to be a vet, too?'

Lewis shook his head. 'No, she wants to work as a graphic artist. She's very talented and she's pretty sure that she'll be able to get work locally when she's qualified.'

Gage pulled in a deep breath. 'I hope it works out well for all of you.' He stood up. 'As Amelie said, we should go now, but we'll see you all again soon, I expect.'

Amelie hugged her brother, and touched her father's shoulder in an affectionate gesture. She smiled at Lewis, and Gage laid a hand in the small of her back, ushering her gently but firmly out of the room.

'What's the rush?' she asked, when they were outside in the corridor. 'You seemed to be in a hurry to get me out of there.'

He winced. 'I can't quite get used to you smiling at him,' he said.

She looked at him in surprise. 'Smiling at who?'

'At Lewis.'

'Whatever do you mean? Why shouldn't I smile at him?'

'Because I'm still having trouble shaking off all my preconceived ideas. I've been jealous of him being near you ever since we first met, and even though he's just told me about his girlfriend, I can't quite get used to the idea that you and he aren't together. I thought he was Connor's father, and I kept telling myself that I shouldn't go near you. I was afraid that I would be breaking up a family unit.'

Amelie absorbed all that as they walked towards the stairs. 'I guessed you might think we had a relationship, but I didn't imagine that you were jealous of him.' Then she thought about it some more and looked at him again. 'So…that means you do care about me?'

'Are you actually asking me that?' He shook his head, before whisking her down the stairs and out of the main doors.

'You didn't answer me,' she said, when they were finally out in the car park.

'Do I need to?' He walked her through there and across the road towards the landscaped gardens opposite. 'I would have thought you must already know how I feel about you.'

'How could I know? Until today, I thought you and Gina had something going.'

'You cannot be serious.'

'I'm very serious. You always seemed to have your heads together looking at something or other.'

'You imagined it,' he said.

She realised that by now they were standing by a bench seat in a leafy arbour, sheltered from prying eyes. She looked around at the peaceful scenery, feeling just a little disconcerted. Why were they here? Didn't he want to answer her?

'I didn't imagine it. I was sure there was something going on. You were so friendly towards one another.'

'That's because she's my cousin,' he said. 'I promised her parents that I would keep an eye on her.'

She stared at him, her eyes widening. 'Your cousin?'

'That's what I said.' He sat down and drew her onto the seat beside him.

'Why are we here?' she asked.

'Because I want to talk to you, and I need time and space in order to think.'

'Oh, I see.'

'And then I thought we might have lunch together. There's a restaurant just a mile or two along the coast road, where the food is mouth-watering and I think you'll enjoy it. Would you like to give it a try?'

Amelie nodded. 'Yes, I think I'd like that,' she murmured, 'but even more than that I'd like to know how you actually feel about me. I don't think I can cope with guessing games.'

He drummed his fingers on the wooden arm of the seat, and then turned to face her. 'I hope you're ready for this.'

She lifted a brow, and he said slowly, 'The truth is, I've been crazy about you almost from the moment I first saw you. I discount that very first time, because I was trying to save your life and I thought then that you were the most beautiful creature I had ever seen. Then I realised that you were beautiful on the inside, too. You were so caring, so good with Connor, and so wonderful to be around.'

Gage frowned. 'You drove me to distraction. I was supposed to be your boss, but I kept wanting to scoop you up and protect you from everything that threatened to hurt you, and then you showed me how strong-minded you were, how you did what you had to do and overcame anything that stood in your way.' He flicked a glance over her. 'And I just fell in love with you.'

'You fell in love with me?' she said.

His mouth twisted. 'I didn't have any choice in the matter, none at all. It just happened, and then when I wanted to tell you how I felt, I realised that Lewis was always around and I wasn't sure just how much of a part he played in your life. I thought Connor was your son, and I was afraid to come between the three of you.'

'He's a friend,' she said, 'a very good friend.' She looked at him and a smile kept trying to break out on her mouth. 'You said you fell in love with me...'

'Yes, I did.' He ran a finger lightly over her cheekbone and across the line of her jaw. 'I love you. I love everything about you.' He was silent for a moment, looking at her. 'Do you think you could love me? I know that you were afraid of being hurt, that you thought every man would turn out to be like your father, but I promise you that I'm not like that. I won't ever let you down. I just need you to tell me that you feel the same way about me.'

'Oh, yes,' she said, her mouth curving. 'I do love you, Gage. I really do. I was fighting it, telling myself that it couldn't be happening to me, but you just came into my life and captured my soul. I want to be with you for always.'

He let out a long sigh, as though he had been holding all the tension inside him. 'I'm very, very glad of that.'

He leaned towards her and kissed her gently on the mouth. 'I want to hold you very tight and kiss you senseless,' he murmured.

'Mmm...' she said on a soft, breathy sigh. 'Me, too.'

He kissed her again and the thrill of his lips pressuring hers sent a fizz of excitement to race through her whole body.

'But first of all,' he said, 'I need to get us out of here, so that I can propose to you properly, in decent surroundings, befitting the occasion. I really want to get this right, because I need you to know that this is for a lifetime, that it's a forever kind of thing.'

'I like the sound of that,' she said. She leaned back in her seat and watched him dreamily. 'I really like the sound of that.'

'That's my girl,' he murmured, kissing her once again. 'My beautiful, forever love.'

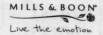

researching the cure

The facts you need to know:

- Breast cancer is the commonest form of cancer in the United Kingdom. **One woman in nine** will develop the disease during her lifetime.

- Each year around **41,000** women and approximately **300** men are diagnosed with breast cancer and around **13,000** women and **90** men will die from the disease.

- 80% of all breast cancers occur in post-menopausal women and approximately 8,200 pre-menopausal women are diagnosed with the disease each year.

- However, survival rates are improving, with on average 77.5% of women diagnosed between 1996 and 1999 still alive five years later, compared to 72.8% for women diagnosed between 1991 and 1996.

Breast Cancer Campaign is the only charity that specialises in funding independent breast cancer research throughout the UK. It aims to find the cure for breast cancer by funding research which looks at improving diagnosis and treatment of breast cancer, better understanding how it develops and ultimately either curing the disease or preventing it.

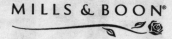

4 FREE

BOOKS AND A SURPRISE GIFT!

We would like to take this opportunity to thank you for reading this Mills & Boon® book by offering you the chance to take FOUR more specially selected titles from the Medical Romance™ series absolutely FREE! We're also making this offer to introduce you to the benefits of the Mills & Boon® Reader Service™—

- ★ FREE home delivery
- ★ FREE gifts and competitions
- ★ FREE monthly Newsletter
- ★ Exclusive Reader Service offers
- ★ Books available before they're in the shops

Accepting these FREE books and gift places you under no obligation to buy, you may cancel at any time, even after receiving your free shipment. Simply complete your details below and return the entire page to the address below. You don't even need a stamp!

YES! Please send me 4 free Medical Romance books and a surprise gift. I understand that unless you hear from me, I will receive 6 superb new titles every month for just £2.80 each, postage and packing free. I am under no obligation to purchase any books and may cancel my subscription at any time. The free books and gift will be mine to keep in any case.

M6ZED

Ms/Mrs/Miss/Mr ....Initials ....
                                                                              BLOCK CAPITALS PLEASE

Surname ....

Address ....

....

....Postcode...

Send this whole page to:
UK: FREEPOST CN81, Croydon, CR9 3WZ